OPERATION VARSITY
The Reluctant Volunteer

OPERATION VARSITY
The Reluctant Volunteer

Monty McGinnis

2025 Tranquility Press

Operation Varsity: The Reluctant Volunteer
Copyright 2025 Monty McGinnis

For information:
Tranquility Press
723 W University Ave #234
Georgetown TX 78626
TranquilityPress.com
TranquilityPress@gmail.com

ISBN 9781950481552

This story is a work of fiction based on real events. Certain long-standing institutions and public offices are mentioned, as well as some real persons; however, they are used in a fictitious manner. The views and opinions expressed herein are those of the characters only and do not necessarily reflect the views and opinions held by individuals on which those characters are based.

Glossary of Military Ranks, Terms, and Abbreviations

Pvt.: Private
CO: Commanding Officer
Sgt.: Sergeant
S.Sgt.: Staff Sergeant
M.Sgt.: Master Sergeant
1st Sgt.: First Sergeant
Sgt. Maj.: Sergeant Major
Lt.: Lieutenant
2nd Lt.: Second Lieutenant
1st Lt.: First Lieutenant
Capt.: Captain
Maj.: Major
Lt. Col.: Lieutenant Colonel
Col.: Colonel
Maj. Gen.: Major General
Lt. Gen.: Lieutenant General

Gen.: General
FM: Field Marshal (British)
DZ: Drop Zone
LZ: Landing Zone

German terms

Achtung: Attention
Luftwaffe: the aerial-warfare branch of the German military during WWII
Reichsminister: literally "empire's minister," a member of the German government, used 1919-1945
Volkssturm: literally "people's storm," an untrained civilian militia
Wehrmacht: The complete armed forces of Nazi Germany

Preface

THIS IS a fictional account of men who volunteered to fly the silent wings of unpowered gliders with a history of high casualty rates into WWII battles.

Leading up to America's entry into WWII, the high command of the Army Air Corps introduced gliders as a tactical weapon. Thousands of men were trained to pilot these lightly constructed aircraft, often called "flying crates" or "flying coffins." They had no armament for protection and flew one-way trips. Gliders carried as many as fifteen troops and/or supplies and weapons to deliver behind enemy lines. Army Air Corps C-47 twin-engine troop carrier aircraft (a forerunner to the DC-3 commercial airliner) towed the gliders into a battle zone, often at night.

When approaching the landing objective, the glider pilot disconnected from the tow plane and glided silently to the ground.

Today these dangerous special missions are the job of highly trained Navy SEAL Teams or Army Special Forces. In WWII, these pilots and troops went stealthily behind enemy lines without special combat training and only a few hours' flight training in the Waco glider. As many as one-third were shot down or crashed, often at the cost of the pilots and troops on board. Those who landed safely moved to secure strategic bridges and roads and engage the enemy until the main Allied armies could advance to relieve them. They contributed to the Allied Forces' success in Sicily, Italy, and Holland and on D-Day.

During the invasion of Germany in late March 1945, the Allied command sent hundreds of CG-4A "Waco" gliders to ferry troops, arms, and supplies over the Rhine River into Germany to secure key roads and bridges prior to the Allied ground invasion. This was a daylight mission over German lines heavily fortified with anti-aircraft guns that targeted their tow planes or the slow unarmed gliders in the air.

To maximize the opportunity of success of this mission, not one but two pilots were required in each glider. Many of these added pilots came from ranks of C-47 pilots. In the last weeks of WWII, the Army Air Corps Troop Carrier Command had a surplus of C-47 pilots and not enough glider pilots to put a pilot and copilot in each glider. Many C-47 pilots volunteered, and some were "volunteered," their names drawn randomly. Many of these "volunteered" pilots had little or no experience handling the unpowered Waco "flying crate" and thought this mission was a suicide mission.

Much has been written about the air war in Europe, the bombing and paratroop drops in critical battles. Not as much has been told about this tactical operation to deliver troops, guns, and supplies over the Rhine River behind enemy lines as part of the invasion of Germany. It was code named Operation VARSITY and resulted in the largest one-day air assault in history.

This fictional story is inspired by the actual service of a "volunteered" pilot who helped make that operation a success.

1. Operation VARSITY:
The Air Assault into Germany

Morning, 24 March 1945

THE ARMY Air Corps twin-engine C-47 transport towing two Waco gliders was in a thick haze of smoke and fog over the Rhine River, about to enter German air space. They left their airbase in France almost three hours earlier. It was March 1945, near the end of the war in Europe. The Allied forces have driven the German *Wehrmacht* army from Normandy, across France and Belgium, back into their homeland.

The C-47 pilot was Lt. Zack Palmer. This was his third major airborne operation, starting with D-Day, June 6, 1944. His plane was part of an air armada making the largest one-day air assault in history. The night before, a ground assault across the Rhine River titled PLUNDER preceded the air assault. Together these operations made up one of the Allies' last major military operations of World War II.

Lt. Palmer's group was near the front of three streaming lines of 1300 C-47s, each pulling gliders from twenty-three airbases in France and England. The troop carrier C-47s would release the Waco gliders, filled with troops, field guns, ammunition, and supplies, behind the German lines, several miles inside German.

While momentarily hidden in the smoke and haze, Lt. Palmer announced to his crew, "When we reach clean air on the other side of this soup, the German anti-aircraft guns will be trying to blow us out of the sky and thousands of soldiers only a thousand feet below will be drawing a bead on us. We're entering their country, their Fatherland, and they will be defending it with their lives. It's their last stand and their *Führer* said it's the last chance to keep the Allied armies from taking their homeland. He's ordered them to fight to the death. 'Throw everything you have left at the Americans and British. Take no prisoners.'"

"Sergeant Smith, radio the gliders," the pilot said. "Tell them the AA guns and small arms fire could take us apart. Buckle up. It'll get a lot rougher."

They cleared the camouflage that was haze and smoke, and the German AA flak began exploding all around them. The black smoke explosions throwing shrapnel into the plane's surfaces took a toll on the big, slow-moving air transport pulling two gliders, each loaded down with almost four thousand pounds of men, field guns, ammunition, and supplies. Their air speed was just above a stall, rendering the big transports easy targets. The exploding flak got closer. The shrapnel tore at the wings and body of the C-47. Rifle and machine gun fire ripped through wings and engines.

"In a few minutes we'll begin our descent to six hundred feet and release the gliders. Dropping that weight will allow us to pull up and away from the intense ground fire and make a wide turn for home."

Their altitude reached six hundred feet a few minutes past the river and the remains of the town of Wesel, leveled to bomb shell holes and piles of rubble from Allied bombing. Lt. Palmer switched on the green release light and instructed his copilot to release the gliders. When he felt the discharge of the gliders' weight, Palmer pulled back on the steering yoke to climb up and turn away from the ground fire.

The number one engine exploded from a hit by a large AA shell and burst into flames. The aircraft shook violently and started to spin out of control.

"Damn, that hit took out our hydraulics. You're going to have to help me operate the rudder and elevators to get back to level flight," he shouted to his copilot and hit the bail-out light and alarm. "Bail out, BAIL OUT," he shouted.

The navigator and radio operator hit their seat belt harness release and were out the side door in seconds. Luckily their parachutes opened about a hundred feet from the ground.

"I'm staying with you, Lieutenant," his copilot said. "You're going to need help manually working the controls. Together we can belly-land this lame dog. You can't muscle it by yourself. I've activated the fire suppression on number one. I hope we don't lose the wing."

One of the released gliders, carrying troops, a field gun, and ammunition, made an S-turn in preparation for an unpowered, dead-stick landing. Flak bursts shook the heavily loaded glider, and small arms fire ripped through its fabric. The glider pilot suddenly shouted, "Damn. I didn't want to be in this unpowered, overloaded crate, but now that we're here and I see what they're doing to us, you Krauts better get ready 'cause there are a lot more of us coming. Your days of killing innocent people and taking countries in this part of the world are over."

The second glider released by the now-crippled C-47 had taken shots from the anti-aircraft guns but was lower and closer to the LZ. The pilot made a dead-stick right turn and lined up to set the heavy glider down on what looked like a stone pathway. He suddenly realized the stones he saw on the ground as a path, was a stone wall. In a last-second move, the pilot pulled the control wheel back, lifting the craft up to clear the wall.

It worked. He missed the wall but put the heavily loaded glider into a stall. The Waco glider nosed into the farmland from about twenty feet above the ground, collapsing the plexiglass nose and cockpit, bending the glider frame, and injuring several troop riders. The weight of its load, the field gun and ammunition it was carrying, broke their tie-down straps and the full weight came down on the pilot and copilot. The first glider came in over the top of the crash site, made a successful dead-stick landing, and unloaded their field gun, ammunition, and troops. The two pilots rushed back to the sister glider to see if anyone survived. Lt. Palmer's C-47 tow plane was fifth in a line of eighty, each towing two gliders. The air assault into Germany was just beginning. A long day lay ahead.

On the ground below, the German army, the *Wehrmacht*, was a fragment of its former size and strength. Three years of fighting wars on two fronts had reduced the *Wehrmacht* army by over two million fighting men. The retreat from the Ardennes Forest in Belgium after Christmas and later a defeat by the British had resulted in the loss of over 70,000 German soldiers. After the Germans retreated across the Rhine in a failed effort to establish a defensive line on the west side of the river, the Führer and his top generals resorted to recruiting old men and teenage boys. There were no more German men of fighting age available to recruit. Only a fraction of available tanks and field artillery were in operational condition. Allied air forces had decimated the *Luftwaffe*, the German air force. The only significant field artillery remaining was the anti-aircraft guns used in the failed defense of the Holland port of Antwerp six months earlier. The Germans quickly relocated those AA guns to the new defensive line on the East Bank of the Rhine. The final defense of Germany depended on the leftover *Wehrmacht* army of 85,000 made up of veteran soldiers, old men, and boys and a couple hundred anti-aircraft guns spread over one hundred miles of the Rhine border.

2. Officer's Mess Tent,
Airfield A58, Coulommiers, France

23 March 1945, 1800 hours

THREE PILOTS of the 72 Squadron of the 434th Troop Carrier Group, Army Air Corps entered the officer's mess for dinner and some light drinking before the planned air assault into Germany the next day. The location was a rebuilt airstrip, A58, at Coulommiers, France, just a few miles southeast of Paris. With over two hundred pilots bivouacked there, they ate in shifts to accommodate everyone.

Friends since final pilot training almost one year ago, the C-47 pilots were eager to eat but anxious to learn about a major air operation scheduled for the next day. They expected a briefing from one of the high-ranking officers in charge of tomorrow's operation.

"Well fellows, I see most of the brass are in here this evening," Lt. Bud Sullivan said. "We should have a plan to draw out the details of tomorrow's operation. Over there, Major Maxwell and Colonel Gavin are eating together. Hopefully, they'll stop at the bar before hitting the sack."

"We may not need to pry much out of them," Lt. William McCallister said. "Notice the crowd around the message board near the back door. I'll bet some of the operational details have been posted. The base has been locked down for several days, no one in or out for security purposes. If you were a spy and wanted to get information to the Krauts, it would have to be sent by smoke signals. Do any of you know any smoke-knowledgeable Oklahoma Indians in this outfit, or any Krauts who can read smoke signals?"

"I hear the bar will close at 9 p.m. and lights out is at 10," said Lt. Zack Palmer, the youngest of the group at twenty-three. Sullivan and McCallister were considered old by the demographic of the hundreds of pilots in the 434th, 435th, and 437th groups of the Troop Carrier Command. One of the top officers of the Eighth Air Force was Gen. Lewis Brereton. The commanding officer of the 434 group at Coulommiers, airfield A58 was Col. Gavin.

As the pilots were finishing the high-calorie meal when Col. Gavin entered the mess tent and stepped onto a pine box and his aide called "Atten-shun." The room of pilots shuffled to a stand.

"At ease, gentlemen," Gavin said. "As you know, tomorrow is the day we take this war to the German homeland. The chow will be open for another hour, and the bar closes at 2100 hours. Lights out at 2200 hours. Get your rest. You'll need it. Tomorrow will be a long day. Briefing in the morning will be at 0600 and wheels up at 0700.

"Posted on the two message boards at the two mess tent entrances are details on Operation PLUNDER, the ground invasion across the Rhine by men of Field Marshal Montgomery's Commandos and Canadian Mountaineers. They will initiate a crossing before midnight tonight, and if all goes well will be at rendezvous locations by midday tomorrow. Those rendezvous locations for pilots are marked on the maps you will receive in your orders envelopes tomorrow morning, along with drop zones and landing zones assigned to each squadron.

"More details and any last-minute changes in assignments will be in the morning briefing. This could be one of the final large-scale offensive operations of this war, and one that will contribute to the defeat and surrender of the Third Reich. Contact your squadron leaders or anyone on my staff with questions. That is all. Get your rest."

Lt. Zack Palmer had already moved quietly toward the dessert table to satisfy his chocolate craving. "I'm headed for dessert, and on my way back I'm going by the message board to see if there's news about any of us or changes in the operation we should know."

Lt. William McCallister was thinking about an earlier operation. "You know, Bud, tomorrow is the anniversary of our resupply of the trapped 101st airborne at Bastogne. Exactly three months ago we were eating and talking about that Christmas Eve resupply trip."

"Yeah, you're right," Bud said. "In fact, there was an operation on the 23rd that resulted in a high casualty count."

"Yes, and we were nervous before going out the next day. That same anxious feeling is back. Tomorrow's operation could be worse. A double tow of overloaded gliders means we'll be flying at near stall speed and low level. Making us a big, easy target for the big German 88 antiaircraft (AA) guns."

Sullivan and McCallister's conversation was interrupted when Palmer returned.

"Hey, you guys need to check out the message board. Promotions are posted, and there's a notice referring to Gen. Brereton's order that all gliders must have two pilots. It states that because there's a shortage of glider pilots, power pilots will be assigned to a glider. Volunteers, especially those with some glider experience, are preferred and welcome."

That got Sullivan and McCallister's attention and they quickly headed for the message board posted at the rear entrance to the mess tent.

Upon seeing the posting they all closely surveyed the promotion letter, which listed officers and non-com promotions.

There were about a dozen names listed under the heading PROMOTIONS TO 1ST LT. Prominent on the list was 2nd Lt. Harry Sullivan.

Neither 2nd Lt. McCallister nor 2nd Lt. Palmer were listed.

"Congratulations, Bud," Lt. Palmer said. "Improved rank, but more important, a raise in pay."

"Yes, congrats, Bud," Mac said. "How did you pull that off?"

"Yeah, I'll take it, even though I'm unsure what I've done different that gets me a bump in rank and not you, Mac, since we've served together since arriving over here."

"I guess that means you buy the beer," Palmer suggested.

"I can handle that," said newly promoted 1st Lt. Sullivan, all the time knowing the beer is complementary, on the US Army before big operation.

When they arrived at the bar, two other officers stepped away, opening enough space for two and three to squeeze up to the rail. Mac was the last to edge up when the tall man next to him moved down to make room. It happened to be Maj. Maxwell, a squadron leader. Mac made a second glance before recognizing his rank.

"Come on in here, Lieutenant Aren't you a little late to the bar? Some of us are way ahead of you guys; which, in my experience, is very unusual."

"Thank you, sir. Yes, were ready for a beer before hitting the sheets." *He looks and sounds like he is way ahead of us.*

Bud turned his head to look at the Maj. "Sir, is everything worked out in terms of pilots to fly the gliders? Did you have enough volunteers to fill the second seat as ordered by General Brereton?"

"Hard to say for sure, mister. We'll have to see who shows up tomorrow for the final briefing. There are often no-shows due to sickness or other that requires some last-minute switching, either of C-47 pilots or glider pilots. I'm expecting we'll need some additional power pilot volunteers to pilot a few gliders before takeoff tomorrow morning. Would any of you like to volunteer?"

"I don't think so, Major, not to volunteer," Lt. Sullivan said. "You may have to order some switches. I don't know any C-47 pilots that would prefer to be towed into an air battle then a dead-stick landing in the middle of do-or-die Krauts. Lieutenant McCallister and I have our usual pre-mission anxiety about flying the big goony bird low and slow over multiple AA guns. And more anxiety, if we are to be towed and dropped in the middle of the retreating German *Wehrmacht*. Any intel on the expected anti-aircraft capability along the Rhine this late in the war? We took a lot of casualties last fall in the Market Garden operation and hope we don't run into the same tomorrow."

"Listen," the Maj. offered. "British Field Marshal Montgomery and General Dempsey directed the Market Garden air operation. It was managed poorly, too slow and inconsistent. Instead of attacking with one concentrated wave of paratroops and gliders, Montgomery sent in planes with ammo and supplies in stages, which gave the Krauts time between to reload, reinforce, and recover. The enemy nearly defeated us on that operation because we had a weak strategy. We're not doing that this time.

"General Ridgeway oversees the air assault and Eisenhower emphasized to Monty and General Dempsey their ground assault must be the lead force. Monty has the well-earned reputation of trying to overpower the enemy with field artillery and air power before he makes a ground attack. Eisenhower made it clear to him the air assault would not proceed tomorrow if their PLUNDER ground assault had not crossed the Rhine by 0600 tomorrow. That should reduce the number of anti-aircraft batteries firing at you tomorrow and clear out much of the enemy on the ground before the gliders start landing at about 1000 hours."

The Maj. continued. "I've had just enough beer to share another story you may have gotten by now about the strategy meeting among Allied top brass a few weeks ago to plan this assault into Germany. Before the top generals met, Montgomery asked Eisenhower for a one-on-one meeting, hoping to convince Ike to choose his, Monty's, plan to make a narrow, spearheaded attack straight to Berlin to kill Hitler, force a surrender, and end the war in a couple of weeks. Eisenhower had sent a memo before the meeting to the top brass outlining his plan to make a broad assault across the Rhine with British attacking in the north, an air assault in the center and General Patton's army coming up from the south."

"Let me guess," Bud said. "Montgomery wanted to lead the way into Berlin and be the one to capture or kill Hitler."

"Maybe so," the Maj. replied. "The story is even more interesting when General Montgomery arrived late to his meeting with Ike, and upon entering the room where Ike was waiting, the British Field Marshall walked up to him pulled Ike's memo out of his pocket, tore it up, and dropped at Eisenhower's feet. Monty reportedly said 'This plan is hogwash. My plan for a spearhead assault straight into Berlin will end the war in less time and with fewer casualties.'

"Eisenhower said, 'Monty, you can't talk to me that way. I am your boss. Now sit and let's talk about the strategy you are proposing.'

"Cheers, Major," I said and held forth my bottle for a sympathetic tap of bottles. "A classy way to put the arrogant Brit in his place."

The Maj. tapped my beer bottle and continued. "After Monty detailed his plan, Eisenhower explained the pros and cons, specifically the danger of the Germans cutting through a narrow assault corridor and, again, trapping our army inside Germany, and the difficulty of recovery from that type of setback. He also explained the broad campaign may not take much longer since the *Wehrmacht* will be spread widely and thinly across the country, making their forces thin on all fronts.

"The strategy allows our several army divisions

to move fast as we push the Krauts back toward Berlin. The Russians pressing from the west also help wrap what's left of the once-powerful *Wehrmacht* in a tight net. I'm only concerned the Russians might get to Berlin first, kill or capture Hitler, and take Germany before we get there.

"Let's see, Sullivan and McCallister. I recall seeing your names on a letter of awards General Williams posted after the resupply at Bastogne," the Maj. said. "Great flying. Well deserved. I'm glad to have you both on our Operation VARSITY tomorrow."

The Maj. turned to Palmer. "Lt. Palmer, I'm Major Maxwell. Don't think we've met. Are you new to the European theater?"

"No, sir. I've been with the 434th flying support in southern France for General Patton's Armored division. Since he's now crossing the Rhine in the south, I was reassigned to the 437th group and the VARSITY operation. Mac and Bud were in my final training squadron stateside."

"Where are you from, Lieutenant?"

"Columbus, Ohio, sir."

"From the Midwest heartland. I hear they grow lots of corn out there."

"Some, but I think you're confusing my state with Iowa. We grow some corn in Ohio but not near as much as they do in Iowa. We are called Buckeye State, and I went to Ohio State University studying accounting. My father is a CPA and has his own business. I hope to join him in the business after the war."

"Is that state nametag due to the planting of buckeye trees a hundred years ago? And, what good is a buckeye nut?"

"Hell, I guess so. And I don't know if they're edible, even with beer."

"How 'bout you, McCallister?" the Maj. continues. "Where are you from?"

"I'm from Kansas, Major. Little corn but lots of wheat, but I live in Kansas City, and work in a casket factory. It's not a dead business, as you might expect. People are dying to buy my product. Right?"

"Right," the Maj. said with a forced chuckle.

"And how 'bout Lieutenant Sullivan? Where is he from?"

McCallister answered since Bud turned to receive congratulations on his promotions from another pilot.

"He's also from Kansas City, a neighborhood friend growing up. He plans to open a hardware store after the war. Says the latest development in home improvement is the window air conditioner. It blows cold air in your house during the summer heat. They're expensive now, but he says costs will come down and every family will want at least one."

The Maj. slid off the high wooden stool and extended his hand to Palmer and McCallister. "You fellas go easy on the beer and get your rest. I'll see you in the morning."

3. The "People's War" and the Volkssturm Recruits

February - March 1945

Hitler and his top generals had come to the realization they would need help from the German citizens if there was any chance of stopping the Allies from taking the country. That need forced the creation of the people's militia named the *Volkssturm* by *Reichsminister* Joseph Goebbels and Henrich Himmler, Minister of the Interior.

They pulled together 750,000 soldiers made up of old men and teenage boys and located them around key cities, preaching to them about being part of the "People's Army" that must fight the "People's

War" to keep the Western Allies and Russians from taking their Fatherland.

The Volkssturm received many of the latest weapons, but not complete uniforms. Uniforms for Volkssturm recruits came from dead soldiers, winter coats from the public, a few steel helmets, and whatever trousers they owned. Each member had to swear allegiance to the Führer, and surrender was not an option.

Hitler dictated a scorched earth policy for slowing down the Allies. He ordered all bridges, roadways, railways, railcars, depots, and canal locks destroyed and issued a "no retreat" order — any man leaving his post will be shot. The *Wehrmacht* regular army officers, in charge of the last line of resistance, tried to position their best troops and anti-aircraft guns where they believed the Allies would attack. The primary job of several thousand Volkssturm militias was in support roles so more experienced troops could move to the front lines.

Assembled in a field northwest of the German town of Wesel was a group of new Volkssturm members. Otto Goetz and Hans Mueller, neighbors from farms nearby, were among the new members of the Volkssturm. Hans Mueller was a pig farmer of big strong German stock, whose property was on a main road northwest of Wesel. He had fifty acres of corn, much of it used as pig feed.

On Otto's smaller acreage north of the Mueller farm, he grazed a few head of cattle. He was a widower with no other family nearby, older than Hans, and a descendant of smaller Austrian ancestry. Their grandparents cleared the land for farming almost a hundred years earlier.

"What are we to do, Hans?" Otto asked.

"No way to know until a general or other officer in charge shows up."

"I see you brought your shotgun, Hans. Do you expect to be shooting at a flock of Americans or just guarding prisoners?"

"Ha. I do not know, but if we are part of the defense of our land, I am prepared. If you want a military gun you would have to go to the front and risk your life taking one from a dead soldier. You did not bring a gun, Otto?"

"Yah, just this Mauser." He held up the German-made automatic pistol. "It will do for guarding prisoners or shooting them. Hopefully, this war is about over, thank God. The Americans and British are only focused on defeating the *Wehrmacht* and eliminating Hitler. They will pass through our land on the way to Berlin. After the war is over, the Allies could hold on to Germany so we can rebuild. We do not want Russia to win and gain control of our country, or we will be speaking Russian and sending our products and our money to Mr. Stalin. Have you heard from your son, Max?"

"Nein; I last heard he was on the other side of the Rhine. His division was retreating from the Ardennes Forest and moving to Schlemm's army in a defense perimeter on the west side of the Rhine. That lasted a few weeks and thousands on both sides died, tens of thousands of German soldiers captured before Schlemm's army retreated across the Rhine into Germany. So, if still alive, he may be close to home again. I expect he is now on the front line of defense somewhere on this side of the river. If we survive these next days, I will try to find him, dead or alive."

A loud *"Achtung"* came from a tall, thin Haupfmann (Captain) named Schultz in front of the group. "You men form three lines." Otto and Hans stepped into the middle of the back line, waiting for further orders.

Haupfmann Schultz continued, "You men are now a part of the Home Guard or Volkssturm army and must demonstrate the same commitment and loyalty the soldiers of the Third Reich have shown in the many campaigns in Europe and Russia. You will not serve on the front lines, but your support roles are also important and badly needed. Every able-bodied soldier can defend the Fatherland from the invading armies. Heil Hitler."

"Heil Hitler," the group of about two dozen recruited German civilians responded.

"Some of you will assist in delivering ammunition to the front lines, others will be preparing food and rations, and still others will be supporting medical personnel."

Haupfmann Schultz turned and started walking down the front line of Volkssturm soldiers now standing at attention, stopping occasionally to adjust a soldier's unkempt, disarrayed attempt at a uniform or inspecting whatever weapon they held.

While inspecting the *Volkssturm* soldiers, he continued lecturing.

"Der Führer has ordered us not to capture enemy prisoners while defending the Fatherland. Captured enemy soldiers will be shot. So, you will not guard prisoners. If any of you are asked to guard prisoners, you must execute them soon after they are turned over to you. Is that understood?"

"Jawohl," a few answered.

"Again, all of you. Is that understood?"

"JAWOHL!" the recruits shouted.

"The Sergeant has your duties and positions. Step up when I call your name."

Otto and Hans quietly listened and responded affirmatively as each part of the civilian group received their assignments. When dismissed, they stepped away to a fallen tree trunk several yards away. They sat to read their orders, regulations, and thought about what had just happened.

"I never thought I'd be drafted into the army when the Führer started this war in Poland," Otto said quietly. "Wasn't your son Max drafted after der Führer invaded Poland?"

"You know, Otto, I hate what it has come to," Hans said. "At one point I thought Germany was stronger than ever and we all would prosper. *Der Führer* was building back our military and economy after the Great War. Then he and his Nazis decided to take over the world. Now I hate what we've become. I just want to be a farmer. I never wanted to take sides in this political war."

"Yes, I agree," Otto said. "It has been difficult to make a living, just holding on to our farm, but I admit after the Great War, I supported the Nazi Party because they advocated building back our strength and image in the world. Hans, we must do our duty now or the Europeans and Americans will take over our land. There will be nothing left for our children and grandchildren."

"Yes, Otto, we will do our duty up to a point. As I said earlier, it would be best if the Americans and British win, because after the fighting is over, they will go back to their homeland. If Russia wins, they will take over this land for themselves and we will be farming for the Communists. I have an idea how we can show support but stay out of the fighting. My land is on the road from Wesel to the Issel River, not very far from here. I'm going to talk to the Volkssturm commander about us setting up an aide station at the farm."

"Good idea; and he doesn't know that's your home. We can be guarding your home as well."

After they pointed out the farm's location on the map, the commander said, "OK. That could be a strategic location for us to stop the enemy from moving up the road to secure the bridges at the Issel River. You men go ahead. I'll send more troops to secure the location."

4. Operation PLUNDER Begins

March 23 0800 hours

WHILE THE pilots at French airbase A58 were talking about tomorrow's Operation VARSITY at dinner, the Germans were becoming more nervous in anticipation of an assault across the Rhine. Several German patrols penetrated the Allied buildup of troops and artillery on the West Bank, hoping to gather intelligence on assault plans. Their efforts learned of an assault, but nothing in detail. German fighter aircraft made multiple strafing runs along the West Bank where British artillery was set up but managed only minimal damage.

By late afternoon of March 23, the Allied forces under Montgomery's command were ready and made final adjustments before initiating the ground assault, code name PLUNDER. At 1900 hours the British command staff transmitted the "ready" code words, Two if by Sea, to all units along the West Bank of the Rhine, and artillery shelling of the German lines on the East Bank began.

At 2400 hours, the first of four waves of British Commandos in small groups entered the river in small boats and within minutes reached the East Bank against light resistance. In less than an hour, two brigades of Commandos crossed the Rhine northwest of the town of Wesel and moved inland within a mile of the town, holding their position while Allied bombers continued to pound the town.

At 0100 hours of March 24, Gen. Eisenhower and generals on his staff positioned themselves in the tower of a church on the west side of the river to observe the beginning of the full-blown assault across the Rhine. The British Commandos laid down a heavy smoke screen over the river, which mixed with a light fog, providing excellent cover for the assault.

The shelling support of 2000 British artillery pieces and additional bombing of inland German airfields wiped out Germany's air capability. A major assault by four British and Canadian battalions behind the massive smoke screen was effective in deterring German defenses. Only three of the fifty-four storm boats involved in the crossing were hit by Germans and only one British soldier was killed. One British officer said the heavy shelling and thick smoke screen thoroughly "cowed the German defenders."

At first light of March 24, two divisions had successfully crossed one of the most imposing natural obstacles in Europe and continued into Germany at the cost of only thirty-three casualties.

The minimal resistance from the Germans allowed two British battalions to form up within forty-five minutes after landing on German soil and begin their drive to the east. Moving inland, the British Commandos found an open seam between two German divisions and encountered light resistance with few veteran German soldiers, allowing them to reach the first railroad line several miles inland.

Not once did the British 79th division have a need to call on air support to meet their objectives. One of the divisions reached the town of Dinslaken, the other pushing back the Germans east of the first railroad line.

By midmorning of March 24, ground forces of British Commandos with Canadian Highlanders had penetrated the German defense line at the Rhine River and were well into Germany when they heard the drone of hundreds of aircraft approaching from the west. The first results of Operation PLUNDER were a success and what the Commandos heard overhead was Operation VARSITY, the largest air assault in history, beginning.

The first planes of the Allied air armada, 2500 troop carriers and gliders, approached the Rhine, delivering over 21,000 paratroops, glider troops, and supplies with support from B-24 bombers and more than 2,100 fighter escorts in case fighters of the

German *Luftwaffe* air force might try to disrupt the assault operations. None did. Another 2500 heavy bombers and 800 medium bombers attacked German airfields, bridges, and strategic targets.

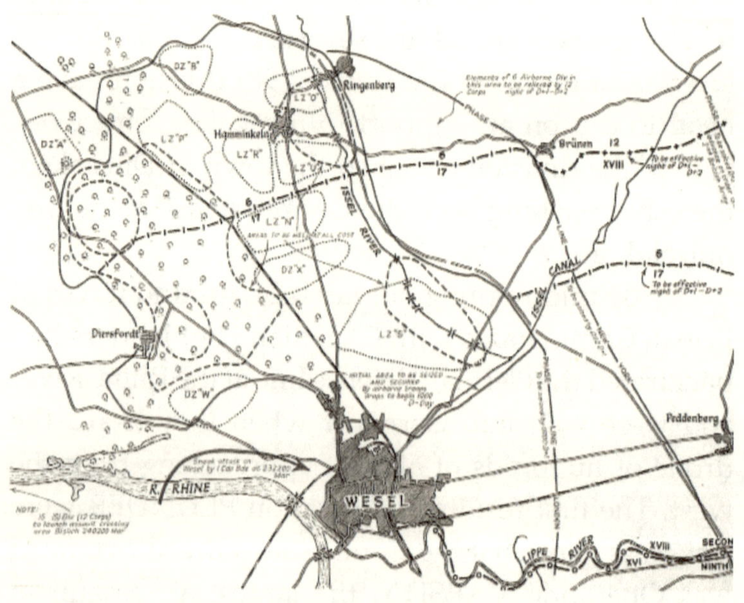

Map of the area around Wesel showing phased objectives for U.S. XVIII Airborne Corps during Operation VARSITY.
On 24 March, paratroopers and gliders under the command of Ridgeway's XVIII Airborne Corps were dropped at zones marked, while Commandos (see bottom left) assaulted across the river on the tight flank of the Second Army.

5. Airfield A58,
Coulommiers, France

24 March 1945, 0530 hours

MY GOOD friend Lt. Bud Sullivan and I entered the huge dining tent at airfield A58 located a few miles southeast of Paris. Over two hundred pilots of the Army Air Corps Troop Carrier Command were consuming a big breakfast, including fresh hot biscuits from a French bakery. Afterward, we expected a final briefing on the day's mission by the Troop Carrier Group Commander, Col. Matthew Gavin.

Details of the mission had been top secret, but scuttlebutt reported it to be a massive air assault over the Rhine River into Germany. The scuttlebutt seemed validated by the eighty C-47 twin- troop carrier aircraft lined up on the apron of the airfield and connected by nylon ropes to one hundred sixty CG-4A Waco gliders, loaded and ready to go.

Yesterday, infantry troops assisted by ground crews loaded each glider with up to four thousand pounds of field guns, ammunition, anti-tank bazookas, mortars, medical supplies, water cans, rations, and jeeps. A second large group of C-47 troop carrier planes configured to deliver paratroops behind German lines lined up behind the gliders and tow planes. Bud and I believed the scuttlebutt of today's mission and expected it to involve many more Allied air groups from bases in France and England.

The briefing this morning would be about finalizing the details of the plan and final orders from the 434th Air Group Commander, Col. Gavin. Bud and I expected to pilot C-47 aircraft delivering paratroops into the interior of Germany to hold key bridges and roads from the German army in retreat. This operation could be the first assault into Germany setting up the final major campaign of the war.

Finally, through the chow line and seated in the large dining hall. "Bud, I can't get the details of our resupply of Bastogne on Christmas Eve out of my head, we flew that risky, low-level resupply drops to the 101st Division trapped in Bastogne with four serials of about fifty C-47s in minimum visibility."

"You're right. That was a difficult and dangerous, and costly, operation, flying under an overcast sky at five hundred and only added only a few days of relief."

"Bud, I'm more anxious about today's operation than I was about that one. There are a lot of similarities, particularly about a low-level daylight raid against lots of ground fire and anti-aircraft guns, big guns."

"I remember well, Mac. When skies cleared, Allied fighters and bombers hammered the German Panzer divisions, forcing a complete retreat. At the time of our resupply, some of the 101st said they had only ten rounds of ammunition left. That mission was an enormous success but costly in planes and pilots."

"That was my first difficult and dangerous mission, Bud, and I didn't really know how tough and dangerous it was going to be. It worries me that we're going to face similar conditions today."

"Yep, you're right, Mac. It was tough, but in the end, we contributed to a big turning point in this war. And as I remember, the Germans' advance stalled because they ran out of GAS. In fact, they outran most of their supply lines of support, including ammunition. Hitler counted on the bad winter weather to keep our air power on the ground, but when the skies cleared on Christmas Day, our air power took over. Our P-51s and Hellcat fighters swooped in and severely kicked the hell out of the stalled Panzers tanks. Combine that with Patton's Fourth Army busting through German lines relieving the 101st airborne and the great German offensive was over."

Bud turned to me. "Yes, Mac, today could be similar; but the German army today is a ghost of the one that surrounded our 101st Cavalry last December. Since the retreat from Belgium and the defeat by Montgomery of their defense on the West Bank of the Rhine, their ranks of veteran soldiers are a fraction of what the Allies encountered during that counter-offensive in the Ardennes. This operation could be as costly as the resupply of the 101st at Bastogne, or it could be easier. The Krauts are not the army they were four months ago. They lost tens of thousands of veteran soldiers in the failed defense of the West Bank and bridges into Germany and are now recruiting old men and boys."

"You're right, again, Bud, but conditions are in their favor again this time. We'll be dragging these Waco gliders into Germany at low levels in daylight. We had to go under the overcast last time, but today we'll be flying at six hundred feet, and slower, towing a couple of heavy gliders."

I can't get Bud excited or concerned with this VARSITY operation. He believed it might be easier than the resupply at Bastogne. I didn't. It was going to be rough.

Lt. Zack Palmer showed up, still consuming a Danish with his coffee. Welcomes and "morning" all around.

"Did you all get any sleep last night? I didn't get much, but I bet the adrenaline will keep me awake all day," Palmer said confidently.

Bud looked at both of us and said, "Are you

all going to volunteer to pilot a glider? I think Major Maxwell was fishing for volunteers last night at the bar. You might be up for promotion if you let him know you'll do it."

"Hell no," I said. "I'm concerned the brass has kept the details of this mission under wraps. I hear they're short of trained glider pilots and are looking for more volunteers from the C-47 pilots. I'm afraid they will reassign us to pilot one of those overloaded cracker boxes. The casualty rate on the Market Garden operation at Antwerp was over thirty percent. Those damn gliders are flying coffins. In training I've towed two at a time, and even in calm air they bounce all over the place. I can only imagine how rough it could be flying in a serial formation with the added turbulence of a long line of aircraft in the sky. Finally, add the potential damage from anti-aircraft fire, and your odds of survival are even lower."

"I didn't fly the Holland mission, but I hear it was a slaughter, thanks to Montgomery's strategy. I'm keeping fingers crossed that I'm still in my C-47 towing gliders. That'll be tough enough," Palmer said.

"Don't worry," Sullivan said. "I hear there are enough C-47 pilots with CG-4A glider training to fill the seats General Brereton ordered. He has little respect for glider pilots, said they were more of a liability than an asset in the Market Garden operation, and because of the high casualty rate and missteps of that campaign, he wants a pilot and copilot in every Waco CG-4A glider. He believes putting more trained power pilots in the gliders will reduce the number of casualties and increase the chances of a successful operation."

"And, he could be right," Bud continued. "But I think he's underestimating the experience and skill of the Waco flight officers. Most glider flight officers are damn good and have proven their skill in glider operations since D-Day. Sure, they don't have as much formal training, but so what? What's important is the skill developed from combat experience. If they've successfully completed several missions under fire and survived, I'd fly with them. You want to get more coffee, Bud? I'm going to fill up and go to the head before the Colonel shows up."

"No. I'll wait for you here." It wasn't that I needed coffee; I just had to walk around. I couldn't just sit there and wait for the rest of the bad news. Plus, I could get another donut. It was going to be a long day with only rations available. I went out to the latrine before returning.

When I walked back to where Bud and Zack Palmer were, they were smiling, even laughing at something. Before I could ask, someone in front of the huge mess hall shouted "ATTEN-SHUN!" Everyone in the room stood up and watched the 437th Group Commander, Col. Gavin, walk to a lectern in the middle of a long table. My watch read 0600 when I heard the "At ease" from the Col.

"Listen up, men." Two M.Sgts. pulled a canvas cover from a tall wall map of Northeastern Europe, France, Belgium, and Germany. Turning to the map and with a long wooden pointer, Col. Gavin slapped it on the large, printed word "GERMANY" in the center. He said, "Today this war moves into Germany. Allied ground and air forces are taking this war across the Rhine River into the German homeland. Earlier this morning, Field Marshal Montgomery's British and Canadian forces initiated heavy bombardment at the German lines dug in on the East Bank of the Rhine River in this area." The Col. swept the pointer along the East Bank of the river north of the German town of Wesel.

He continued, "Those ground forces crossed the Rhine River just after midnight this morning and are moving inland from this area at this hour." He pointed to the Rhine north of the village of Rees on the wall map. "This ground assault is code named Operation PLUNDER. A combination of British Commandos and Canadian Highlanders moved across the Rhine River headed for their first objective, the town of Essenden, a few kilometers inland. Our Third Army, led by General Patton, crossed the Rhine River here." Col. Gavin tapped his pointer on the Rhine south of Wesel, near Dusseldorf.

I leaned over to Bud and whispered, "Scuttlebutt this morning indicates the Brits crossed the Rhine without any major resistance and very few losses."

Col. Gavin continued, "Squadrons here at Coulommiers airfield will join with air squadrons from other bases in France and England to deliver troops and armament across the Rhine, dropping into

Germany to protect strategic sites from retreating German forces. This air assault operation, code name VARSITY, will join with either British or American land assault forces. The goal of forces delivered by VARSITY is to secure strategic crossroads and bridges to enable ground forces of PLUNDER to move inland with minimum resistance. Certain squadrons of C-47 aircraft will carry paratroops, and others will double-tow Waco gliders loaded with troops and support equipment, medical supplies, and ammunition. En route to the Rhine, our air group will join with air groups leaving from twenty-two other airfields in France and England at a rendezvous point over Belgium." The Col. tapped the pointer on Wavre, Belgium. "These groups will merge into three serial lines spaced one and a half miles apart and adjust course for the run to the Rhine River and into Germany."

The rumbling of hundreds of pilots talking about the day's operation created a dull roar. The Col. continued the briefing.

"All right, quiet down. Give me your attention. We have briefed your squadron leaders, and they will deliver your orders along with maps of your route and designated drop zones for paratroops and landing zones for gliders. Read them and take the time to understand your part. Commit as much as possible to memory. Your squadron officers or my staff will answer questions. Glider pilots need only get their aircraft on the ground, then move to one of the pilots' rendezvous locations on your map. The British and

Canadian ground forces of PLUNDER will relieve you within thirty-six hours. Troop commanders and artillery teams have orders on the unloading and movement of weapons and other supplies."

The Col. paused and an aide set a mug in front of him. "Any questions at this point?" he asked and took a sip of what I presumed was coffee from the mug.

The room was silent so he continued. "C-47 pilots who did not receive an order packet, see Major Maxwell against the wall to my right for your orders. Every pilot on this base will have a job to do, and success depends on all of us executing our jobs to the best of our abilities. The successful execution of today's Operation VARSITY will spell the eventual defeat of the Third Reich and the end of the war. This day's combined Allied air forces will be an armada of 1500 powered aircraft, and 1300 gliders headed to the Rhine River and into Germany. Three hundred P-47 Thunderbolts and P-51 Mustang fighters will escort us. Gentlemen, you will be part of the largest combat air assault in history."

The Col. paused a moment, then dropped his pointer loudly to the table. "Finally, a word of caution. This is not like landing in France or Holland. When you meet a civilian, remember they are German, even if not in uniform. Do not assume they are friendly just because they dress like civilians. Joseph Goebel and Heinrich Himmler have conscripted old men and boys into the army, calling them Volkssturm, or Home Army, and emphasized to them that this is the last stand to save the Fatherland. German military clothing, equipment, and guns are in short supply. Not all these Home Army are in uniform. So, beware. Assume all the Germans you meet will try to kill you."

He paused again to let that sink in, then concluded. "When you have your orders, move out to your aircraft. The first aircraft off this field will be C-47s towing gliders. Troop carriers will follow. First in line, be ready for wheels up at 0700. That is all. Good hunting and Godspeed."

The squadron officers shouted out names over the din of hundreds of pilots asking questions all at once. A M.Sgt. nearby with an armload of brown envelopes called out "Lieutenant Harry Sullivan."

"Over here," Bud shouted, waving his hand.

After several names comes "Lieutenant Zack Palmer."

"Here." He waved.

I followed Zack to see what his assignment was while waiting for my name to be called.

"I'm towing with a pilot I've flown with before, and we're in position five, near the front of the serial. I like it," Palmer said. "Go ask him if he has orders for you, Mac."

I did and he didn't. *What the hell? Am I not flying today? That would be too good to be true. He told me to go see Sgt. Boyle or the Officer of the Day at a side table.*

When I joined about a dozen pilots around the table, I heard someone call my name from behind me.

"Lieutenant McCallister." It was Maj. Maxwell.

"Yesterday I saw your name on a list of power

pilots chosen to be glider copilots for this mission," he said. "I didn't tell you last night because they hadn't finalized the list, and I knew you didn't want that change. I was hoping you would not be on the list this morning."

"What's going on, sir? I'm going to assume someone must fly the bird I've been flying for weeks. Why isn't he assigned to copilot a glider? What did I do to deserve this assignment?"

"This is not a punishment, Lieutenant. The committee making these changes are trying to match up the best pilot and copilot teams, taking the necessary number of power pilots to get two pilots in every glider. As a copilot, this will not be a ride-along, but a long, turbulent flight, so I expect you will get all the flying time you can manage. Adding your experience with an experienced Flight Officer in the glider is an important part of the strategy to maximize the success of today's mission."

Bud walked past me, Zack Palmer following him. "We're headed outside for fresh air and a smoke. Did you get your orders? Carrying paratroops or towing gliders?" he shouted.

I didn't answer, shrugging my shoulders in an "I don't know" posture.

"See you at the back door," Bud said.

All the pilots at this reassignment table were 1st and 2nd Lt.s, power pilots like me assigned to gliders. I didn't recognize any of those guys from earlier assignments, and none of them were in the resupply of Bastogne, as far as I could recall. From their looks and their starched fatigues, some were rookies.

The Officer of the Day got everyone's attention around the table. "Good, everyone should have their orders. These are a change from your usual assignment. Most of you know General Brereton ordered every glider to have a pilot and a copilot for this important mission, and he issued that order knowing we are short of trained glider pilots. Since the order was issued, we have put many power pilots through glider training but found we still need more pilots to maximize the use of our gliders for the delivery of arms and supplies. So, a committee of senior officers matched your names with glider pilots with like combat experience to fill the remaining vacancies of glider pilots. These new orders match you to a specific glider and pilot, depending on your and the glider pilot's experience level."

It made no sense that an experienced power pilot was "volunteered" to be a glider pilot. He said "matched" but I bet it was just names picked out of a hat. Luck of the draw, period.

"Most of you will serve as copilots because the C-47 pilots with glider training have already filled empty pilot positions. However, you will not be just a ride-along copilot, as this flight to Germany is approximately three hours long and due to the number of aircraft in serial formation, turbulence will be a challenge all the way. Both pilots will get plenty of flying time under difficult conditions. I know this is unexpected, a last-minute surprise. We are confident each of you can fill this vital role and make this mission a success."

I knew I could fly; it's soaring over enemy lines in an overloaded crepe-paper glider I was afraid of.

"Thank you for accepting this assignment to change seats and pilot a different aircraft at the last minute. I know your glider pilot is thankful for your help. I'll wait for questions after you open and read over this change of orders."

I opened the orders envelope and confirmed the assignment: Waco glider Chalk 36. I was assigned to copilot a CG-4A glider.

Another C-47 pilot said, "You're assigning us to a duty most of us have not trained for, and on a very dangerous mission. We know the casualty rate of Market Garden. Piloting these crates in daylight at low altitude, through flak-filled skies, and small arms fire, is a high-risk job. If half those overloaded crates reach the ground safely, a German machine gun nest will pick off pilots and troops before they can get out the glider door. I respectfully request my original C-47, or a C46 pilot assignment."

I wanted to say "Damn right. Put me back into my C-47."

Before I got up enough courage to agree with that pilot, the Maj. had a firm answer. "Denied. You don't have a choice, Lieutenant. Move out according to your orders or you will be confined to base."

Several pilots looked around for someone else to object, to speak up, but the silence meant we had no choice. Maybe we all realized it was part of being a soldier, trained to follow orders regardless of the peril we might face.

The Maj. continued, "As you head to your assignments, pick up an additional weapon from Sergeant Miller on my right. You all have a side arm, but once on the ground and confronted by the enemy, you'll need more firepower."

I looked over the choices and selected the Thompson submachine gun. I qualified as an expert shot with a carbine but wanted more fire power as there was likely to be close combat after we landed. The Thompson was covered with grease for protection from water and mud and had two extra magazines strapped to it.

We all exited the mess tent through the side door leading to the airfield. Outside I found Bud and Zack smoking Lucky Strike cigarettes.

When Bud saw me, he spoke without pulling the cigarette from his lips. "What's the story? What is your assignment?"

"Copilot in a CG-4A glider. You were wrong, Bud; there's not enough glider pilots or power pilots with glider training to satisfy Brereton's order. So, the brass made a random selection of C-47 pilots to make up the shortage. The Major threatened one power pilot with insubordination when he objected. We had no choice if we want to stay out of the brig."

"No shit. Damn." He tossed the lit cigarette to the ground and crushed it with his foot. "A bum rap, but you can do this, Mac. They picked the right pilot."

"Correction. Copilot. I'm the ride-along," I

said.

"Yeah, but this is a long flight to the Rhine and your pilot will want some relief. I'm betting you'll get your share of flying, and more. Don't sell yourself short, Mac. You're an excellent pilot and you'll get through this. Paired with an experienced glider pilot, you can be a successful team. Besides, I don't care what the brass thinks of glider pilots. Those who have survived this war so far are not just washed-out power pilots. Their lack of formal training means nothing at this point. They're now the best at flying these bricks with wings, or they wouldn't be alive today. Cut 'em some slack and work with 'em. Keep an open mind and work as a team. You can get through this."

"I agree," said Lt. Palmer. "And, believe me, pulling those heavy gliders at an air speed just above stall makes the C-47 a much bigger and easier target for the German AA guns. We're just as vulnerable, if not more so, than the gliders."

I listened and realized my friends made sense. Their common sense logic was encouraging. Palmer was younger, but wise for his age. He was right about the C-47 being an easier target, flying low and slowly pulling heavy gliders. Who said I was safer in a big C-47? Still, once they've cut the gliders loose, the transport planes can return to base. The glider pilot must land and fight his way back to base.

And Bud. He was like a big brother, two years older, and the poster boy for the Army Air Corps pilot. Confident in all things, and there was no job he couldn't manage. He stood over six feet tall, square jawed, lanky, with a flat top burr haircut, and wiry strong. When not smoking Luckys, he chewed gum, popping it at will. When ready for another smoke, he saved the wad by sticking it behind his ear, of all places.

Physically, I wasn't even in Bud's league: two inches shorter, less muscular, with a receding hairline, and more calculating in my choices regarding all things. I smoked, but chewing gum made my jaw sore in two minutes.

His rank was 1st Lt., and he received the promotion on his first eligibility. We enlisted at the same time and I was still a 2nd Lt.

"C'mon, Palmer, we've got to find our birds," Bud said, pulling a wad of gum from behind his ear and tossing it in a wide-open mouth. "You're towing today, right, Palmer? Where are you in the stream? Earlier, I heard you mention number five. If that's true, you need to be starting engines about now."

"Yep, I've got to get out there. Good luck, Bud, and you too, Mac. See you back at the bar."

"Good luck, my friend," Bud said as he shook my hand. "I'll see you back here in a couple of days. I'll buy the beer."

He turned to leave, then turned back. "Oh, I almost forgot, this is for you." He pulled a small revolver from his hip pocket. Holding it in the palm of his hand he explained, "I picked up this little revolver from a critically injured member of the Belgium underground who was going home."

As he spoke, he held the firearm out to me in

the palm of his hand. "The Belgium underground made these revolvers as a backup weapon in case of capture. Notice its folding trigger, no trigger guard, and snub nose barrel, making it small enough to hold and conceal in the palm of your hand. If you're captured, pull it from your pocket before they search you and hide it by turning your palm inward, or to one side, showing only the back of your hand."

He held the pistol with his hands up, the pistol to the side, palms out.

"Available for use at the opportune time when you can get the drop on your enemy. It carries five rounds of a caliber larger than a .22 but smaller than a .38. It's loaded, and because you'll be searched, you don't want to be caught carrying more rounds in your pocket. Here, take it. You'll be on the ground and may need it more than me."

"Are you sure, Bud?" I exclaimed. "I can't take this. It's your extra weapon and you might need it."

"No, not today," he said. "I'm dropping paratroops and coming back here. You'll need it more after you land, if you're caught by the Krauts. I've got to go."

"You're a great friend." I shouted as he sprinted away. "I won't forget this. Good luck."

I put the small revolver in my back pocket and continued reluctantly toward the flight line with a scowl on my face and my eyes to the ground, avoiding the well-meaning comments from my fellow C-47 pilots. Nearing the taxiways of the airfield, I looked up to see two long, straight lines of unpowered Waco gliders parked between two lines of C-47 mother ships like soldiers waiting for duty. It was a damp cold morning, and Europe had a wet Spring. The wet tarmac and runway suggested we had an overnight shower.

This was going to be a long day. Maybe my last day? I was volunteered by drawing my name from a hat to pilot an aircraft I'd never flown before on one of the most dangerous missions of the war. I was feeling sorry for myself when a voice called from behind me.

"Lieutenant McCallister?"

I slowed my steps and turned my head to see a short, stocky, younger man walk up beside me, his arm and hand offered in front of me.

"I'm Flight Officer Jerry Griswold, your pilot today."

I stopped at his blocking arm and shook his thick hand. "Good morning, Mr. Griswold." His youthful appearance was as startling as his cheery attitude.

Great, now I've got to ride second seat on a suicide mission with a gung-ho glider jockey.

"Follow me," he said. "I was out here yesterday watching the troops load our Waco and found her fit for duty and ready to take the fight to the Krauts on their home ground. As you know, spacing the load in these light-weight airframes is important. If the heavy load is not well balanced, we could nose in on takeoff."

We approached the gliders. Jerry asked, "Are

you qualified in a glider, posted any time in the Waco?"

"No" I said sharply. My mood prevented a cordial response. Jerry led me to the Waco CG-4A glider with a large "36" written in white chalk on the side.

I stopped in my tracks, staring at what I was about to get into. *I've towed two of these gliders at a time in training but have no training or experience piloting a Waco glider.*

My anger was showing. I was still struggling to accept that I had to fly the damn thing in combat. For me to copilot a Waco glider instead of tow was a demotion, a slap in the face.

Was it a punishment, and not just the bad luck of the draw?

I'm a ride-along pilot in an overloaded paper-wrapped crate with two tons of men and armament, about to fly into Germany through exploding flak from anti-aircraft guns. Then, possibly, execute a dead-stick landing in a farm field filled with German troops. It's a suicide mission. I'm older than most enlistees, married with two children, and joined the Army Air Corps to avoid fighting the enemy hand-to-hand on the ground. After two years of training to qualify as a multi- military pilot to deliver troops and supplies to our infantry, today I'm headed for the hand-to-hand ground combat I worked and trained to avoid.

"Lt. McCallister," Jerry said as we stood next to Waco glider number 36. "I know you feel you got a raw deal, and you'd rather not be on this dangerous operation in a Waco glider, but I'm glad to have an experienced pilot with me in the right seat. This is my third glider combat mission, and, believe me, I wish you could have been with me on D-Day at Normandy or in the Market Garden Holland assault. Most glider pilots flew those missions without a copilot, and believe me, we could have used your help, your skills, maneuvering these gliders to safe landings."

"Yeah, I'm sure you know others call it a flying brick or flying coffin."

I turned and looked him in the eyes. I'm sure my stare was an angry one and Jerry's pleasant demeanor turned stone cold, likely due to my negative comments about gliders in general. He was about as angry as me. But the reputation I spoke of came from the documented history of those gliders coming apart in training exercises. I'd made double pulls of Waco gliders and knew how they bounced around in turbulent air. The Waco was simply a steel air frame wrapped in coated aircraft fabric, like fabric used in WWI biplanes. It had a thick plywood floor, but no engines, no defensive guns, no armor to stop a rifle's bullet or shrapnel from exploding anti-aircraft flak.

"How many hours do you have in the C-47?" Jerry asked.

"Maybe a hundred."

"When did you arrive in the European theater? Any combat experiences?" he asked, opening the side door of Waco 36.

"I arrived in England six months ago. I've

made several resupply runs and delivered paratroops on two missions. I made two low level resupply trips, dropping para packs of supplies to our guys trapped in Bastogne last Christmas Eve."

"Wow, Lieutenant. Say no more. I'm sorry you feel you're in a more dangerous situation today, but I don't care how you got here. I am glad you're with me," Jerry said. We were still standing at the side entrance door when Jerry extended his arm, directing me into the glider.

"After you, Lieutenant You'll have to slide sideways around the jeep to get into your copilot seat. This jeep and its mounted thirty-caliber machine gun and four troopers are our primary load."

I followed his direction but turned back after taking the copilot seat and saw a smile on his face. He said, "Both of us have a better chance of coming back

C-47s and gliders ready for takeoff

Above: Pilot and Copilot at the controls of a Waco (Silent Wings Museum)

Below: C-47 with tow rope and communications Line (Silent Wings Museum)

in one piece."

6. Takeoff from Airfield A58, Coulommiers, France

24 March, 0700 hours

No doubt I'd insulted the young, qualified Flight Officer. Still fuming and considering the infancy of our relationship and the shocking events of the morning, I didn't care. Jerry reminded me of a typical glider pilot recruited from a construction job or driving a truck. He was irritated by my negative attitude. Many other power pilots like me were angry, thinking of that mission like a demolition derby of old stock cars. The goal of the contest is to be the last car still running — but even the last car running is mechanically destroyed.

Jerry Griswold was two or three years younger than me with a strong stocky frame and calloused hands implying a construction or truck driving job. He wore a campaign jacket with sheepskin lining, an aviator's head cover, and thick-soled work shoes. All except his flight jacket and cargo pants were personal clothes.

The glider pilot learned flight skills from a few hours of classroom and a half dozen hours of glider landings at one of three stateside airfields. Many entered glider training after washing out of power pilot training. Their actual flight training included several unpowered dead-stick landings on a paved strip or open field. They graduated as Glider Pilot, not commissioned officer. Combat-experienced pilots earned the title Flight Officer, and most by that time in the war had completed several missions, starting with the D-Day operation the previous June.

Landing a Waco glider with no power had one advantage over power aircraft. The fabricated glider had a larger wing area, allowing for longer glide slopes than a power plane. Unfortunately, in combat situations, carrying a maximum payload of two tons meant shorter glide slopes, less time to find a landing spot, and no second chance, no go-around and try again if you overshot or undershot the landing.

I'd towed Waco gliders in training and knew their history as tactical weapons in several campaigns since D-Day. The glider proved its value by successfully delivering heavy guns, ammo, gasoline, and medical supplies to ground troops that powered aircraft couldn't drop undamaged from higher altitudes. The glider had a larger wing area and a fraction of the weight of powered aircraft, thereby a lower wing load per square foot, allowing it to land at a lower speed into small fields. The Waco gliders had a fixed rolling gear for runway takeoff and landings, plus skid rails next to the landing gear reinforced with heavier wooden "skis," enabling it to slide over muddy or frozen ground, likely conditions we would face today.

Buckled into the copilot's seat, I did the few preflight checks necessary. Jerry pointed out the five basic instruments available: an altimeter, air speed indicator, compass, rate-of-climb gauge, and bank-and-turn indicator. Many flag officers in the Army Air Corps argued that a compass wasn't necessary because the tow plane with full instrumentation was towing the glider to the drop zone.

Jerry unbuckled and strode back to check the jeep tie-downs and the troop riders. Satisfied all were secure, he reported through our communications hard line connected to the tow pilot that we were ready for takeoff. We heard the 1200 horsepower Pratt and Whitney engines of the first groups warm up then taxi to the main runway, followed by a louder roar of the first departing groups taking off. It would take more than two hours for all 80 C-47s with gliders to get airborne and we were near the front, glider number 36, wheels up expected in about thirty minutes.

"You said you arrived in theater after Market

Garden, Lieutenant McCallister. If you don't mind me asking, what were some of your assignments before the supply drop at Bastogne?"

I turned and looked straight at Jerry. "Call me Mac; and Jerry, I'm not mad at you. I apologize to you for my sour mood. As you've figured out by now, I didn't volunteer for this assignment and it's not just inconvenient, it's crap. Some committee of brass drew my name from a hat for this job. I was volunteered to pilot a glider without advance warning, let alone training, in the most vulnerable aircraft in service. It's my first day in a Waco glider, required to do on-the-job training on one of the most dangerous air missions of this war."

I looked over at Mr. Griswold and our eyes met. "I am a damn good C-47 pilot, and I'd bet a fifth of scotch my replacement today isn't as capable. Flying the C-47 is also a tough and dangerous job, with little more protection than these crates, but I'm experienced and have successfully piloted the C-47 in combat and in all weather. None of this assignment makes any sense to me."

I eased off my rant. "Now that that's off my chest, I promise you my best effort helping you fly this fragile crate." I checked and snugged my seat belt harness and sat back, ready to go.

"Believe me," Flight Officer Griswold said. "I understand. This was not my choice either. I wanted to fly fighter planes. I qualified for flight school but washed out. How or why is not important, but that failure put me in this glider."

Jerry Griswold continued his pitch. "I'm proud to have successfully completed two combat missions, D-Day at Normandy and Market Garden, retaking Holland. I'm as good a glider pilot as any, with combat experience to back that up. You power guys have a copilot to assist and back you up.

"Until today, the troops riding in the glider were totally dependent on one pilot. Many troops lost their life because they lost the pilot and there was no backup. I've wrestled this crate to a safe landing under enemy fire in two major missions without a copilot. So, I was sincere when I said I welcome your help. With my glider experience, and with you as copilot, we both have a better chance of survival, a good chance of going home in one piece."

The more he talked the more I empathized with him and realized he was right. I needed to commit to the situation and make the best of it. I leaned back in my seat and looked over at Jerry as he finished his comments.

"Someone once told me a successful mission outcome depends on skill, smart decisions, and luck. Together, I think we can score high on the first two, which will improve our chances for luck and survival." With that, Jerry extended his open hand to me.

He was right. I realized Gen. Brereton was also right. With two experienced pilots, the gliders carrying big guns, troops, ammunition, and medical supplies had a better chance of getting their precious load safely to the infantry on the ground. I just didn't want to be the one to prove that out. I also noticed earlier that morning that I wasn't the only power pilot assigned to a glider.

I reached across and shook his hand. "You're right, Jerry. I'm with you. Let's make it work. I meant to ask you. Do you know the crew of our tow ship?"

"I know the pilot is Captain Warren Danforth, nickname Sky. I understand he's seen action in several operations starting with D-Day. He's older than me, like you, and he hails from Michigan. Don't know his copilot, likely a replacement."

Our tow plane rolled forward, taking up the slack in the thick rope. The nylon tow rope that connected us to our C-47 had a 30 percent stretch before tightening up. When the slack was out, the first few yards before we moved was like stretching a rubber band. Our tow plane moved forward, following the gliders and aircraft in front of us to the main runway. When the slack and stretch were out, the line went tight, and we were pulled along.

To avoid in-flight collisions, the two gliders' tow ropes were of different lengths, the shorter about 350 feet long and the other 450 feet. When the stretch was out on both gliders, we were all roaring down the old French runway. The C-47's two Pratt & Whitney s screamed at max power trying to pull the heavy Waco gliders off the ground. Our airspeed indicator showed liftoff at 90 mph, and we quickly rose higher than our tow plane. I knew from my experience piloting the C-47 that it had to exceed 100 mph to lift off. When it did, the tow plane just scraped the top of a line of trees at the end of the runway!

We quickly reached our cruising altitude of 1500 feet in a line of planes called a stream behind seventeen tow planes and thirty-four gliders. The buffeting rough air hit us immediately, created by a quartering head wind trying to push us off course and the prop wash of the leading C-47s and gliders in front of us. It became a jarring turbulence like I'd never experienced in the C-47 or in several training double-tows. Some called those gliders silent wings, but the roar of the twin-engine tow planes ahead and noise from the buffeting wind and fabric cover flapping around the glider's steel frame required shouting between pilot and copilot even through our intercom headsets. The turbulence caused our tow plane to bounce around, adding to our own battle with crosswind and turbulence. I tightened my seat belt, forgot about the actual battle ahead of us, and began to worry about whether we'd hold together long enough to get to the Rhine River and Germany.

"Mac, we've got over two hours of this rough ride. I suggest we trade off taking control. Are you with me?"

"Yes; again, forget what I said before takeoff. I'm with you. We've got to work together. I'm going to hold lightly on the control wheel. Let me know

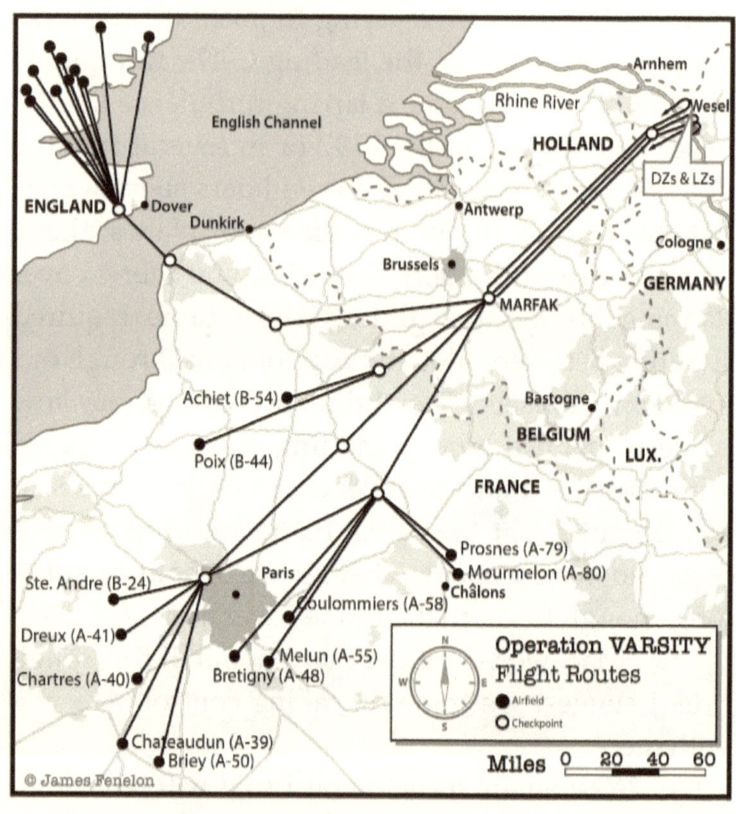

when you need relief."

Map of routes to Germany, March 24, 1945 (From James Fenelon's book *Four Hours of Fury*. Used with permission.)

Above: Operation VARSITY, en route in a CG-4A glider

Below: A C-47 towing two Waco CG-4A gliders

7. New Orders at Airfield A58

24 March, 0645 hours

EARLIER AT Coulommiers field, the C-47 paratroop carriers were positioned behind the gliders. Their lighter loads allow a faster air speed, enabling them to pass the C-47s towing gliders on the way to the Rhine. Bud Sullivan approached his C-47 "bird" from the rear. Paratroopers were checking their gear and lining up to climb aboard the C-47s.

The troops wore infantry clothes of heavy canvas pants with leg-side pockets, cotton canvas shirt, lined canvas jacket, and leather gloves. They wore paratrooper boots buckled high on their ankles for support. Helmet chin straps cinched tight. Most carried the semi-automatic .30 caliber M1 carbine, smaller and lighter than the M1 Garand, the standard infantry weapon. The squad leaders carried Thompson machine guns.

Bud expected to be flying paratroops since that had been his assignments until now. He did not like the possibility of a tow assignment because it meant a slow tow of the heavy gliders into the teeth of anti-aircraft flak and small arms fire while dropping to the low altitude of 600 feet before disconnecting. The big C-47, flying low and slow, was a bigger target with no defense capability. The only protection for the four-man crew was an airframe wrapped in sheet aluminum. Its large wings held aviation gasoline, their most vulnerable spot.

He thought about McCallister's predicament in a glider copilot seat. Bud had never flown the Waco glider, and he was thankful the staff officer's committee hadn't chosen him to be a glider pilot. Piloting the glider was not difficult. It was a fabric-wrapped frame, usually carrying over a ton of troops and armament. It was the most unprotected of all aircraft. Even if the pilot made a clean landing without the frame busting apart, he then faced a deadly enemy and wished he had more infantry training.

It wasn't just about physical training and weapons training. When a trained soldier goes into battle, he has had weeks of training to equip himself for his role as a foot soldier confronting his enemy face-to-face. Pilots without combat training have been known to go into shock when confronted face-to-face with the enemy. Bud knew some could not face it, including those who could not face this mission today. The thought of getting shot out of the sky or gunned down after landing safely could be unbearable.

Approaching the troop carrier aircraft, he noticed two other pilots standing near the nose of the C-47 talking to a Sgt. carrying brown packets like those handed out earlier. When he reached them, the Sgt. turned toward him. "Lieutenant Sullivan?"

"Yes, I'm Lieutenant Sullivan. What's up, Sergeant?"

"Major Maxwell ordered me to find you and give you this order packet. I believe it's a change in aircraft. This is Captain Lewis and Lieutenant Brown, now assigned to this aircraft." Handing the envelope to Bud, he continued. "Captain Danforth, originally assigned to the C-47 tow plane noted in this envelope, was reassigned to a B-24 that lost its first officer to illness."

Bud opened the orders thinking about his friend McCallister's predicament, reassigned to a glider copilot seat. Now he was changing aircraft at the last minute. Reading the orders, he wasn't happy to learn the change was to pilot a C-47 tow plane. The assigned C-47 towing two Waco gliders was located near the center of the serial line of 80 tow planes and their gliders. It made him wonder which C-47 was towing McCallister.

I didn't see his orders or ask him where he was in line. Nah, I doubt I'm pulling his glider. It's an eighty-to-one chance.

He was thankful that the pilot reassignment

was not to a glider for this operation, but flying the largest target in the sky was no cake walk. Piloting a fabric-wrapped glider into enemy territory was not difficult, but still more dangerous, without power and more vulnerable than any other military aircraft.

Disappointed and irritated at the riskier assignment, he accepted this last-minute change without complaint. "OK, gentlemen I'm off to fly a tug. See you later." Bud tucked the envelope under his arm, stood tall, and walked briskly across the airfield to find his tow plane. Since the C-47s loading paratroops were staged at the end of the taxiway behind the line of C-47 tow planes and gliders, he had a long walk up the line of eighty C-47 tugs.

When he arrived at his newly assigned aircraft on the port side near the door, he noticed a pilot walking around the plane. He looked over to the other side of the aircraft to see the gliders stacked nose-to-tail, connected by nylon ropes to the tow planes, or tugs, in the center of the taxiway.

His eyes couldn't quite tell through the many nylon ropes which two gliders were theirs, chalk numbers 33, 34 or 35, 36. Like many war planes, a creative crew painted this one a unique name, "Georgia Gal." A pinup of a beautiful woman posing in a red swimsuit adorned the side of the aircraft just behind the cockpit.

Bud approached a familiar-looking tall, thin officer he recognized from an earlier operation looking much like the copilot, walking around the aircraft doing the preflight checks. "Is that Harry

"Legs" Hunt doing preflight checks for me?" Bud said.

"I am your man. Is that Bud Sullivan?" First Lt. Hunt replied and walked to him with an outstretched hand. "There's no one I'd rather fly with than you." Shaking Bud's hand, he continued. "I've nearly completed the preflight checks, and our Georgia Gal is about ready to go."

"Did you name this beauty, Legs?"

"No, the original crew named her with the pinup painting. You'll notice she's got a few patches here and there. She took a beating at Market Garden and her original crew, including the pilot, were injured but recovering out of the hospital, they're doing well, I understand. So, we get to fly the Gal today."

"Good, looks like we're near the center of the serial, about twenty minutes before wheels up. I'll meet you in the cockpit and we'll warm this girl up."

Taller and thinner than Bud, the younger copilot was observing working elements of the big C-47, checking the landing gear, flaps, elevators, gas tank vents, doing mandatory routine preflight inspections. Harry's curly hair matched his thin red mustache barely distinguishable among the freckles on his tanned skin.

He got the nickname Legs during basic training for his dubious ability to hold more beer than bigger, overweight pilots in the air corps. He had the reputation of never losing a drinking contest, a physical attribute commonly known as having hollow legs.

Bud greeted the other two crew members, Lt. Dan Coffman, navigator, and Sergent Tom Campbell, radio operator. When Lt. Hunt came aboard, they grouped together near the flight deck and Bud spoke to his crew.

"The initial challenge for us will be to maintain our position, separated in formation; and since we're near the middle of the serial, this will be a rough flight. We expect a northwestern crosswind and the buffeting of prop wash from gliders in front of us.

"When we reach the rendezvous point, merging with hundreds of aircraft from other airfields in England and France, there is the possibility of collision of Allied planes and/or gliders, and we do not want to be one of those. I will need your eyes and ears to watch for dangerous movements all around us on our trip to the Rhine River.

"Furthermore, there will be heavy anti-aircraft fire as we cross the Rhine, and then we must drop to about 600 feet before releasing our gliders, during which time we will be most vulnerable and may need to take quick evasive action once we are free of our tow-load. Questions?"

Crew members were nervously apprehensive about the long flight and day ahead. Plus, the pilot was a stranger as they prepared for a big dangerous mission. No questions.

"Sergeant Campbell, get on the comm line to the gliders. I understand communication can become unreliable from dragging the line on the ground during takeoff. Let's be sure it's working from the start. If we do encounter some static, I need you all to listen with me so one of us understands the scratchy communication."

After preflight checks and questions, their expressions showed serious thoughts and fears as one by one they walked to the olive-drab colored tail dragging C-47 and climbed the two steps up and through the side door.

Bud went to his seat, buckled up, and turned to his copilot. "Legs, light 'em up, let's get this show in the air."

Lt. Hunt called out his window to the ground crew, "Clear on number one, ready to start." The ground man signaled with a thumbs up. Lt. Hunt pulled the throttle lever open about ten percent and threw the power switch. The propeller began to rotate, and the coughed out a cloud of black smoke as the big radial spun up in a steady, loud roar. The same procedure occurred on two and soon both were winding up in a loud, low-pitched hum.

The first twenty C-47s leaving Coulommiers Airfield A58 were warming up and within minutes moved into takeoff position. Because of the number of tow planes and gliders, the lineup extended onto the main airstrip. This shortened the available runway for the first several planes in line, presenting a challenge to get tow plane and gliders off the ground high enough to clear the tree line just off the end of the runway.

Lt. Zack Palmer and his crew were fifth in line and the reconstructed French air strip looked way too short for his liking. He pulled out the slack in the tow rope, then the copilot set the brakes. He pressed the power levers to max and revved both 1200-horsepower engines to full power. The pitch of the props was slowly dialed in before the brake was released. With the shorter runway, it seems too slow to reach to the lift off speed of 100 mph, but they got up to speed with wheels up in time to just clip the treetops at the end of the runway.

Within minutes, almost half the tow planes and gliders were off, and Georgia Gal started her roll down a longer runway. Her two big 1200-horsepower radial engines screamed at full power, lifting all three aircraft off, easily clearing the treetops at the end of the runway. Within a minute they reached cruising altitude of 1500 feet in a serial line headed northeast to the Belgium rendezvous point. Upon falling into the serial line, they immediately began to suffer the buffeting prop wash of the first C-47s and gliders. A strong quartering headwind trying to push them off course added to their difficulty maintaining their altitude and position.

"Coffman, have you worked out our ETA to the rendezvous mark over Belgium?" Lt. Sullivan asked.

"A few minutes less than two hours, Lieutenant, assuming we can maintain the current ground speed against this quartering headwind and prop wash buffeting."

"Campbell, how are the gliders doing back there? Keeping their separation?" Bud shouted into the intercom. "Are you able to communicate with them? Do you know the pilots?"

"Yes, Lieutenant. Separation is good but they are dancing like butterflies out there. The comm line is clear. I know the pilot on the short rope is Lieutenant Roy Lee Smith, a veteran of both D-Day and Market Garden. He has a new copilot I have not met. The pilot on the long rope is Flight Officer Jerry Griswold, a veteran of D-Day and the Market operation. I don't know his copilot. The comm line has some static but it is working. I can tell they are struggling to maintain separation and are holding at a higher altitude to avoid the turbulence. The noise in the glider must be deafening. They've been shouting in the com line because of the background noise of the fabric slapping on the glider frame. I hope those crates hold together in this turbulence. It 'll be a rough ride to the Rhine."

C-47s towing Waco CG-4A "Waco" gliders

8. Gliders to the Rhine River

24 March, 0800 hours

I WAS irritated and disgusted by our inability to consistently exchange information clearly with the pilots of our tow ship. The hard communication line between the gliders and tow ship was wrapped around the tow rope, and often got damaged before takeoff from dragging on the runway. A scratchy voice transmission was the norm, if there was any at all. During much of the flight we dangled out on our own with only visual signs to direct our movements.

We were at the mercy of our tow ship's instability, jerking us around while we also fought turbulent air coming from the line of planes and gliders in front of it. The wings vibrated violently, and the tail fluttered up and down. Jerry tried maneuvers to stabilize the tail, "before it breaks apart," he said. The accumulating chaos heightened my worries about the ability of the crate to hold together long enough to get to the Rhine.

While tightening my seat belt, I looked over my shoulder to see if our two-ton load was still secured to the floor. The sight of the straps on the jeep stretched tightly to the glider floor calmed me for a few seconds. My eyes roamed back to the few gauges on the tubular instrument panel in front of me while both hands remained on the control wheel.

Our heavy glider swung up and down, back and forth like a backyard tire swing in a thunderstorm. Jerry wrestled the control wheel, trying to hold the bucking, swinging two-ton crate behind the tow plane and away from our sister glider only yards away from our tow rope. I was impressed with Jerry's control skill and determination. His white-knuckle grip on the control wheel told me he had all he could manage to keep us on course with good separation from our sister glider.

"Jerry," I shouted. "I never asked you who's flying our sister glider. Do you know him?"

Instead of an answer, I got a long silence. Before I could raise the question again, he shouted over the continuing roar of multiple engines and the loud slapping fabric.

"Can you take her for a few minutes? This is the roughest ride I've ever had."

"Yes, I've got it," I answered.

Thirty minutes into our trip we hit a downdraft that pushed our crate down at least twenty feet. Muffled groans emanated from the riders in the back. We later learned several tossed their breakfast into air-sickness bags due to the severe turbulence. Usually, I wasn't sensitive to air sickness, but that was the roughest air I'd ever encountered.

We continued flying east in our serial group of eighty C-47s, pulling twice that number of gliders. I spelled Jerry at the controls every fifteen or twenty minutes as we approached the rendezvous position over Wavre, Belgium, where serial flights from over twenty other airfields in France and England were converging.

We were looking for ground markers to determine our position when we entered a low-hanging cloud bank. Our tow plane disappeared. All I saw was about a hundred feet of our tow rope. The crosswind faded, but turbulence from aircraft in front of us still whipped us up and down.

"Ok, Mac. I think we should try to drop our altitude to see if we can get under this cloud layer."

"Agree, let's do it; and we should try to maintain the same angle of dangle of our rope from the tow plane, meaning no side angle as we drop."

"Wow, look what just showed up," I said as our sister glider dropped out of the cloud layer in front of us, only a few feet to the left of our tow rope.

"Right turn, Mac. We gotta move away from Barry's short rope. I doubt he sees us behind him."

"On it. I see him. We're sliding right."

I made the move to the right and breathed more easily when our tow plane dropped below the cloud layer and we saw the gliders in front of him. Without any formal communication, the whole serial group dropped to an altitude of 1200 feet.

Soon we reached the rendezvous point at Wavre, Belgium. The serial line of troop carrier aircraft and gliders merged with similar groups from English bases and serials from nine bases in France. All merged into three parallel lines of troop carrier planes, planes towing gliders, bombers, and over nine hundred fighter escorts. The aircraft armada stretching back west hundreds of miles and covering the north-to-south horizon began a turn east on heading 090 for the Rhine River and Germany. Our eighty C-47 tow planes and gliders merged into the third serial of the armada now heading due east for Germany. If you were standing on the ground looking up at the stream of aircraft, it would take two hours and thirty minutes for all the aircraft of the armada to pass over.

A total force of 21,000 men, armament, and supplies made up the massive air assault, code name Operation VARSITY. At the preflight morning meeting, pilots received maps of drop zones for paratroops and glider landing zones on the east side of the Rhine River near the German town of Wesel. This was the second phase of the Allies' two-pronged assault into Germany.

At 1010 hours we started to see exploding flak from enemy anti-aircraft guns near the leading planes and gliders and as they approached the Rhine River. There was a wall of thick smoke and haze over the river. We knew the British generated smoke to cover their Commandos crossing the Rhine in boats. Within minutes, we saw the West Bank of the river just ahead as the leading planes in our serial cleared the Rhine River. Flak from the German anti-aircraft guns got heavier. The leading tow planes started dropping below us and began releasing their gliders. The landing zone assigned to us was LZ-S, a ten-square-mile area north of the town of Wesel.

As we came through the thick smoke over the river, flak from the anti-aircraft guns and small arms fire intensified. The first planes in our group dropped to the release altitude of six hundred feet. We watched the first in our group take hits from ground fire. The small arms fire and shrapnel from exploding flak ripped the fabric around the fuselage and wings into confetti. We followed the first group a few hundred yards behind. *Ready or not, here we come.*

We all braced for the deadly ground fire we were about to take. I was on the control wheel over the Rhine planning to turn it back to Jerry to make our landing. I wrestled the control wheel, fighting the turbulence and incoming fire. I knew Jerry had been in this situation, battle tested, and hoped he would be ready to take back control when we cut loose.

The concussions from flak added to the turbulence as we passed over the Rhine. Shrapnel continued ripping the fabric of our wings and fuselage. I began this mission with a sour attitude because the brass "volunteered" me to copilot the overloaded crate, but there was no time to whine about it and my thoughts turned to our troop riders taking fire.

A scratchy voice came through the communication line from the tow ship. "Gentlemen, we are approaching the release altitude and will be giving you the green light to release momentarily."

I turned to Jerry. "You said a Captain Danforth was piloting the tow ship. That voice is familiar to me. Sounds much like a buddy of mine I thought was flying paratroops."

"I'm sure it's Captain Danforth," Jerry said. "I talked to him last night."

"Okay but you know the way they shuffled pilots at the last minute. Makes me think it could be my friend, Bud Sullivan."

The cut-off green light flashed.

"We have the cut-off light, Mac! I'll take it from here. You can release the tow rope from our end. Thanks for your help. I can get us safely on the ground."

I unlatched the tow rope and watched it drop away, and I watched our sister glider's tow rope drop away. We were on our own. It was the precise time we needed Jerry's landing skill. I eased off the control wheel but maintained a one-handed grip. The twin-C-47 tow ship pulled up in a wide turn. Free from two heavy gliders, it easily gained altitude for the return to base.

Envy and anger enveloped me immediately. *I should be in that cockpit.*

That was my job, piloting the C-47, not riding in some unpowered glider. My duty in this war was flying the C-47. I recognized that bird with the pinup girl on her nose. I'd brought that plane from England to our French airbase last week. Why wasn't I flying it today? Instead, I was copiloting an overloaded glider hoping I didn't have to make my first dead-stick landing behind German lines.

As I continued watching the C-47 bank in a wide left turn, an AA shell exploded on its left engine, setting it on fire and forcing it out of the turn. The big plane leveled out just as another shot hit its tail.

Damn, I sure hope Jerry was right and Bud isn't in the cockpit.

"Did you see that, Jerry? The damn AA guns hit our tug twice. He'll be lucky to get down safely. The pilot is still trying to keep it in the air."

He completed the turn and headed for home base. They'd lost some ability to maneuver but still had one good engine that could keep them in the air for a while, but not enough power to gain the altitude necessary to get back over the Rhine and back to base. It was difficult to go very far without gaining altitude.

He's too low to bail out. He has to find an open field to put her down safely and away from German troops.

Above and below, views of

Landing Zone S near Wesel

9. Georgia Gal en Route to Germany

0930 hours

TIME SEEMED to crawl while all crews battled the crosswind and turbulence. Finally, they met with serial flights from England and French fields over Belgium and the air armada turned due east for the Rhine. In less than an hour they saw smoke and haze on the horizon. Bud and Legs knew they were approaching the Rhine.

"I bet the Brits created that smoke to cover their troops crossing the Rhine. Smoke from their fires combined with humidity from the river to make a thick cloud, a barrier cloud in front of all three approaching serials," Bud said. "It will give us cover for a minute or two over the river, but when we break through on the other side, the Krauts on the East Bank will be all over us."

He glanced at his watch. The hour was 0945 and the lead flights entered the smokey haze at the Rhine River, over a mile wide. As they got closer, the Georgia Gal pilots could see the additional black puffs of smoke from German anti-aircraft guns peppering the sky among the descending power planes and gliders being cut loose as they descend below one thousand feet.

"We'll begin our descent after we cross the river and reach clear air on the other side of the smoke and haze. At six hundred feet we will adjust our heading for LZ-S," Bud announced over the intercom. "I will give them the green light as we get closer to LZ-S. They might cut loose sooner if they need to. If we get hit by AA flak, we will cut them loose from here.

German AA guns were hammering the two other serial lines of planes flying on Georgia Gal's left flank just before they entered the smokey haze over the river.

"Here we go. Buckle up; it could get rough."

Bud dropped the nose as they entered the smokey haze. Upon clearing the smokey barrier at the West Bank, the AA flak and small arms fire from the ground intensified. Shots pinged off the wings and fuselage. At six hundred feet, the plane was east of the river and the pilots saw smoke rising from the rubble of the town of Wesel, Germany, the result of constant shelling from Allied air forces.

Bud adjusted his heading to 020 degrees

northeast toward LZ-S, then lit the green cut-off light. When he felt the release of the gliders, he pulled the nose up and put the C-47 aircraft into a tight left turn. The big aircraft's left wing dipped in response just as two quick hits from a German AA gun struck the left engine hard, rolling the whole aircraft upright. Another lucky shot made a direct hit to the tail.

Bud and copilot Hunt wrestled with the control wheel to maintain a level flight. Then a flak explosion shook the right side of Georgia Gal's fuselage and shrapnel penetrated her midsection, tearing into Navigator Coffman's legs. Another near hit blew fragments into Sgt. Campbell's back.

On the flight deck, Bud said, "I'm trying to feather number one ."

"It's smoking and leaking oil badly." Lt. Hunt replied. "I will free-wheel the prop. Do we still have power on number two?"

"Yes, and I'm going to let it pull us into a 180-degree turn and we'll try to head back over the river."

"Lieutenant Sullivan," Coffman shouted in the intercom. "We've taken shrapnel hits from the last flak. I've got a shrapnel in my leg and Sergeant Campbell took shrapnel in his back and head. He's bleeding badly and unconscious. We need to get down and find a medic."

"Damn. OK, I hear you, Coffman," Bud said. "That last shot on our tail disabled our elevator and took out our hydraulics."

Harry reported, "Lt., I don't think we have enough power to gain altitude or make it back across the river. We're dropping below five hundred feet. Getting too low to bail out. The best bet is to head for LZ-S. Look for a big flat field near the landed gliders to set her down and get the boys to a field hospital."

They passed over LZ-S noting over two dozen Waco gliders spread out in various positions on the ground. Some were intact, others in pieces.

"I see a long narrow field northwest of LZ-S," said Lt. Hunt, pointing to a clear field next to a line of evergreen trees. "We need to stay on this side of those trees. The Issel River is on the other side."

"I'm not getting any response trying to lower the gear," Bud said. "Those flak shots for sure took out our hydraulics. The ground looks too rough for the landing gear anyway. We'll take her in on her belly."

They tried to come in parallel to the trees, but the damaged control surfaces and minimal hydraulic pressure made straight-and-level flying very difficult. Upon ground contact, the running right engine dug in and twisted the airframe into the line of trees, shearing off the wing and spinning the fuselage to a stop facing the tree line. Before they had unlatched their seat harnesses, a German machine gun cut loose on them from a small house at the end of the field, less than a hundred yards away. Fortunately, the torn-off right wing left a gaping hole in the fuselage facing away from the small house.

Lt. Hunt was first out of his seat. He reached Coffman. "Put your arm around my neck. We'll slide out the hole left by our torn-off wing." He helped

Coffman up and out through the opening while the German machine gun ripped a string of penetrating shots the length of the fuselage. Its shells easily penetrated the air frame and hit Bud, following the others, and knocked him through the opening. Another shot hit Sgt. Campbell for a second time while he was still at the radio.

Outside, Lt. Hunt noticed Bud's injury. "How bad are you hurt, Lieutenant?"

"Shot in my back and shoulder, but I can still move. The ricochet off the fuselage took some of its power. I can crawl over to those trees for better cover. How is your leg, Coffman? Need help with the tourniquet?"

"No, I've got it under control," the navigator replied. Another burst from the Germany machine gun tore through the fuselage again.

"I'm concerned about Sergeant Campbell. We need to get him out of there," Bud said. "Do you think he's alive?"

"Yes, we should," said Lt. Coffman, "but I'm afraid he is not alive. He took a shrapnel hit and a second hit from the machine gun."

"I didn't get my Thompson, but I think I can reach Lieutenant Coffman's," said Hunt, crawling back in the torn-apart aircraft and reaching for the machine gun on the floor.

"See if you can get the first aid kit next to your seat," Bud shouted.

Lt. Hunt was able to grab the Thompson machine gun and the first aid kit while Bud and

Coffman were limping and crawling toward the trees. Bud had his machine gun strapped around his neck, pulling himself along on his right side. He groaned at the pain emanating from the back of his left shoulder. When they reached the first large tree, Coffman sat up against it and said, "Drag over here, Lieutenant Let me look at that shoulder."

When Bud reached the large tree, he turned on his side with his back toward Coffman. Coffman said, "I can see where the shell penetrated your jacket but there is only a blood stain. I don't see any serious bleeding. You just got a superficial wound and a fat bruise from that shot. Penetrating the fuselage took most of the force of the bullet."

Lt. Hunt reaches them with the first aid kit. He tosses a bottle of aspirin to Sullivan and took charge of the injured leg. Coffman's shrapnel-injured leg was more severe than Bud's shoulder. Hunt began by tearing the pant leg away from the wound, then opened a package of sulfa powder and sprinkled a generous amount on the gash, opened a gauze pack, pressed it on the wound, and wrapped a roll of gauze tightly around it. "That will slow the bleeding. You will need to loosen that tourniquet every few minutes to allow blood to circulate."

Hunt, Coffman, and Bud Sullivan huddled to discuss their next move. They all wanted to check on Campbell, who might still be alive, but it was too dangerous to go back into the wreck for him. First, they needed to neutralize the heavy fire from that German machine gun.

10. Gliders Landing in Germany

24 March, 0930 hours

THE FASTER C-47s carrying paratroops had arrived in Germany and delivered their paratroops to the designated drop zones when the Germans first heard the rubble of the leading tow planes approaching the Rhine. As the low flying C-47s passed through the smoke and haze over the river, the German gun crews experienced the rumbling noise change to a roar and saw overhead the massive armada of planes covering the sky. They started firing hundreds of rounds per minute, turning their gun barrels red hot.

A German AA battery commander had just started chewing a fat German sausage when he heard the rumble of the Allied air armada approaching from the west. The sound turned into a thundering roar directly above him as hundreds of planes appeared overhead in a staggered formation spread south to north as far as he could see. He watched in shock and awe for a full minute trying not to choke on a mouthful of sausage.

Snapping out of his awe-struck trance, he quickly gulped down the sausage and ordered his gunners to take aim at the biggest planes in the sky. The anti-aircraft guns were *Flakvierling*, preloaded four-barrel, 20-mm guns capable of firing eight hundred rounds per minute and rotating 360 degrees to easily track the lumbering C-47s pulling gliders. The rapid-fire bursts included a tracer round, which the commander watched explode on the right and wing of a C-47, breaking the wing in half. The plane spun out of control toward the ground. Gliders in tow cut loose and continued east. The C-47 and pilots nosed into the ground in a spectacular crash, sending up smoke and fire.

There were so many aircraft, another German anti-aircraft gun commander later recalled, "We didn't have to aim at one plane; gunners just pointed to the sky, kept firing, and made many hits." After firing thousands of rounds, the gunners replaced the four red-hot barrels with cool ones, firing armor-piercing, incendiary, and explosive rounds.

The same anti-aircraft batteries had engaged with the British Commandos in the early morning and now found themselves under fire from multiple directions, including troops and artillery landing behind them. Some AA commanders lowered and rotated their guns to ground level and fired directly at the attacking British Commandos.

An AA gunner screamed to the battery commander that his gun would no longer rotate. The commander rushed to the gun pit and saw the pile of empty shell casings stuck in the base of the gun, preventing it from rotating. The gun operators stopped firing to help their commander pull the jammed empty casings out, freeing the gun to turn around. The crew swapped out hot barrels with cool ones preloaded with their last rounds. The commander recognized they were out of ammo. He grabbed the radio and called the supply depot. When a British voice answered the phone, the German commander dropped the radio. He knew there would be no resupply of ammo. The enemy was closing in.

Jerry and I were free of the tow plane and concentrated on setting a course to our landing zone. At a lower altitude, we were in more stable air and Jerry started a turn northeast toward our landing zone, LZ-S. He leveled out at six hundred feet. We continued to take enemy ground fire but the flak from the AA batteries was less at the lower altitude. Quietly soaring inland from the East Bank of the Rhine, I reached into my jacket for the landing zone map. I thought for a moment about what our commanding officers said at the morning briefing.

"Pilots and troopers, you have at least two

additional concerns. First, there are no friendly farmers. Assume all civilians will fight for Hitler just like his soldiers. Remember, we are an occupying force, not a liberating force. Second: Hitler has issued a no-prisoners order on the eve of an assault. Captured enemy soldiers will be shot on sight.

The black and white map issued at the morning briefing showed ground markings of the landing zone. It also marked power lines in our path, which appeared much farther ahead. The ground came into clear view and rifle fire picked up. I felt like a big pheasant soaring over a corn field trying to avoid shotgun fire.

Jerry finished the turn on the final heading as we took more ground fire that penetrated the fuselage, pinging off the metal glider frame. Our troop riders had been quiet, indicating no serious injuries so far. Our sister glider on the shorter rope released in front of us and banked right.

KABOOM! A concussive blow shook the heavy glider violently. The plexiglass below our feet and plywood floor between our seats exploded, creating a windstorm of wood, plastic splinters, and metal shrapnel tearing at in the cockpit. Instinctively, I turned away from the storm and looked down to see if I'm hit.

No pain, no sign of physical damage, and the aircraft seems to be intact. We are still airborne.

Jerry cried out, "I'm hit, Lieutenant! Take control."

I looked over to see him holding a shredded and bleeding right arm. Glancing down to the floor, I saw only the ground flying by beneath us. Momentarily, my left hand joined my right hand holding the control wheel steady. Then I reached for a first aid kit under my seat. *Yes, it's still there.* I pulled the zipper bag to my teeth, ripped it open, and handed it to Jerry.

"There should be gauze and sulfa powder you can use to help stop the bleeding. Don't worry, I can land this thing."

I saw some Wacos on the ground up ahead. We might have found LZ-S. But it was crowded; there wasn't enough open ground to make a safe landing.

I looked left about ten o'clock and saw an open field that looked good. While turning left I watched for a farmer's stone wall or hedgerow, which could destroy the fragile Waco, but saw none. Jerry instructed in a calm voice, "If you continue your turn another five or ten degrees, you'll see an open field large enough to set down safely." Just then a stark reminder came to mind again.

This is my first glider dead-stick landing. One shot, no going around again, no second chance. So what! I can do this. I'm a trained pilot and have done this many times. Ignore all the noise, the shaking of this cracker box, and the ground fire trying to rip us apart. Hang on, hold steady, and make this landing. Do it.

Pointing the glider to the open ground, I leveled the glider's descent to less than a hundred feet.

Thank God there's no fence or stone wall on the approach. Just an earthen berm and fence at the other end. Ignore them; concentrate on setting this crate down, making a smooth landing.

Considering the appearance of plowed and muddy ground, I wanted to set the aircraft on its wooden skids, keeping the nose from digging in. I eased back on the control wheel and the glider nose held up, no stall, gliding easily at less than ten feet above ground, committed to land. The small arms fire quieted. My concern was getting us down and stopped. We were about to touch down when I saw two anti-aircraft gun barrels sticking up above the large berm in front of us. They fired rapidly at our incoming planes.

When the anti-aircraft gun commander dropped the phone and turned his attention back to the AA gun, a large movement appeared in his peripheral vision. Turning left, he stared more intently and saw a strange aircraft with a wide, rounded, clear glass nose skidding toward his gun pit, spraying mud in front of it. The shock of the odd-looking enemy aircraft skidding toward him stirred his fighting instincts. He stepped to the top of the berm surrounding the pit, drew his Luger sidearm, and began firing at the aircraft, hoping to stop it before it plowed over him and the AA gun battery. The AA gunners firing at the planes circling above did not see or hear the skidding glider approaching.

Jerry was encouraging. "You've got it, Lieutenant, hold steady now." He turned his head around and shouted to the troops in the back. "Sergeant, be ready to jump out when we stop, and try to neutralize the enemy AA gun up ahead. Lieutenant, release your harness so we can get out as soon as we stop."

Bill McCallister, you have ably flown the powerless Waco glider to a successful landing onto the cold muddy German farmland, sliding in the mud on the glider's heavy wooden skids.

I no longer had control and didn't know if the heavy glider had enough momentum to hit the gun pit. The only thing stopping us was the drag from the fixed landing gear slicing through the mud. The skids and front plexiglass nose pushed up the mud like an ocean wave as we plowed forward. I could only watch as the AA gun in front of us continued to fire at the Allied planes overhead. Both Jerry and I saw what looked like a German officer, maybe the gun commander, on the edge of the berm above the anti-aircraft gun pit, firing a pistol at us as the glider was about to hit the berm. We ducked as the German's bullets splinter the plexiglass nose only inches in front of us. The glider slowed but I knew we would hit the pit.

The glider ripped through a hog-wire fence and punched into the berm, stopping only yards from the AA gun. The wave of mud sprayed forward, striking the pistol-firing German officer, who stumbled and fell back into the gun pit. The AA gun, louder now, continued firing, thump-thump-thump. The side door of the glider swung open, Sgt. Frank Bolton leaped out, and in one motion he pulled the pin of a grenade and lobbed it into the anti-aircraft gun pit. The explosion killed or severely wounded all the AA gun crew and the gun fell silent.

When the other troop riders jumped out of the glider to check on the gun crew casualties, they took enemy gunfire from a hedgerow about fifty yards to the right of the glider. The enemy fired at us in the cockpit and fuselage hoping to kill anyone inside. Their bullets passed through the fabric-covered craft, ricocheted off the steel frame, some hitting the jeep, others passing through, just missing troops exiting on the other side.

I'd already released my seat harness, so I turned to help Jerry with his badly wounded right arm and release his harness. Enemy shots ripped through the side of the glider's plexiglass nose. Jerry threw off the harness and ducked down near what used to be the glider floor but was now muddy ground due to mud splattering through the open floor during landing. The gauze wrap on Jerry's arm reduced the bleeding, but I could tell the arm was in bad shape and needed medical attention.

The troop riders took positions on the berm and returned fire at the hedgerow. The Sgt. directed a squad of three men to circle the pit and flank the enemy while providing cover fire. The Germans retreated into the woods with the American squad in pursuit.

I helped Jerry up, around the jeep, and out the side door, then found a splintered piece of wood from the exploded floor to wrap and stabilize Jerry's injured arm. One of the troops handed him a scarf. "Here, use this for a sling to hold his arm."

Several troops grabbed the tail of the glider and pulled it away from the berm, turning it ninety degrees, moving the nose and cockpit away from the berm. They propped the tail up using two wooden support legs the glider carried. Then the troops rotated the plexiglass nose assembly up and locked it in place to enable Sgt. Bolton to roll out the jeep with its mounted 30-caliber machine gun.

The troop riders followed Sgt. Bolton in the armed jeep heading east to their regiment rendezvous site. Jerry and I sat together looking at the map to determine our location and mark a path to the pilot's rendezvous location. Laying his compass on the map indicated the direction to be two hundred degrees northwest, five or six kilometers away.

Our sister glider landed about fifty yards away in the same field. Their troop riders followed our troops, and we saw the two pilots walking toward us.

"Howdy, Lieutenant. I'm Roy Lee Harrison and this is my copilot, Barry Krawitz, a recent replacement glider pilot. He's been hit with shrapnel from flak shots and needs a medic. Yesterday he was tagged as a greenhorn. After our successful flight and landing, you can address him as Flight Officer Krawitz. I asked one of our troops to go back to LZ-S and to find a medic."

I stood and extended my hand. "Bill McCallister, but you can call me Mac. Glad to meet you, Lieutenant Harrison and Flight Officer Krawitz. Congratulations on the successful landing. Now if we can all get back to base it will have been a successful day. This is Flight Officer Jerry Griswold. He was also injured when we took an exploding AA shell in the belly. Lucky we all got down in one piece. He also needs more medical attention as soon as we can find a medic or get to an aide station."

Lt. Harrison said Barry Krawitz hailed from Brooklyn and just arrived in Europe a couple of weeks ago. Map in hand, Roy Lee pointed out the rendezvous location on the map, pointing to the southwest. A medic came running and examined both pilots. He put a fresh bandage on Jerry's arm and discovered Krawitz's injury to be more serious.

Jerry was moving more easily and said he could continue with us to the rendezvous. The medic said Barry Krawitz needed to get to a field hospital. The medic gave both injured pilots a shot to ease their pain. Krawitz stayed with the medic and three of us headed for the pilot's rendezvous point at a crossroad shown on the map.

As we moved out, I turned to Roy Lee. "You sound like you're from Texas, Roy Lee.

"Yep, from Dalhart. Know where that is?"

"I do. Panhandle, north of Amarillo. How did you manage to get this sweet assignment?"

"During the Market Garden operation, our number two took a hard hit by an AA gun just as we released the paratroops. The direct hit took out the engine and collapsed the wing. We had to bail out. When we hit the ground, a nearby machine gun nest killed my copilot and navigator. I managed to avoid the enemy until I got back to Allied lines but never got a replacement plane. While waiting, they ordered me to glider training. They have more CG-4A gliders than C-47s at this time in the war. I suspected I would be reassigned to fly the glider this time."

We stopped against a stone wall to rest. "How about you?" he asked me. "How come you're piloting the crate and not towing?"

"Probably like you, too many pilots, not enough power aircraft, and a shortage of glider pilots. I was one of many power pilots volunteered this morning by the brass without any prior training. I was assigned as copilot and mad because I thought I was going to be a ride-along. As it turned out, we both had plenty of work to do. I expected to be a tug pilot because of my experience towing these crates. Never expected they would put me in one.

"Turned out a smart decision by General Brereton. Jerry is an experienced glider pilot, but his injury might have taken the glider down if I hadn't been there. This morning, a C-47 pilot friend of mine thought there were enough volunteer power pilots like yourself with time in a glider to fill the open seats. Not so, as it turned out."

"We better keep moving and keep an eye out for the Krauts," Roy Lee said.

"Yes, even though I have avoided being

face-to-face with the enemy," I said. "We're not on the front line but we've landed in the middle of the war."

Roy Lee, Jerry, and I moved west quietly, coming up behind a five-foot-high hedgerow of stones and thick bush. German farmland was randomly divided by stone walls put together using native rocks and hedgerows of thorny vines, making it difficult for four- and two-legged animals to go through or over.

Peeking over the top, we noticed German troops moving across the farm field next to us. "Let's follow this hedgerow to the end and see if we can turn northwest again. Try to avoid those Krauts moving east. Stay low and as quiet as possible," Roy Lee said. He led us, stooping low, opposite the German troops. Roy Lee and Jerry carried an automatic rifle nicknamed a burp gun because of the different sound it made when fired. Together we were well-armed but none of us wanted to challenge the German troops.

Within minutes we saw the stone rubble of a church and adjoining graveyard. Moving closer, we heard multiple shots, different sounding shots. Keeping our cover, we crept closer to find a group of pilots had cornered some Germans in the bombed-out church with only three partial walls and no roof. The Allied pilots had the enemy surrounded in the church, but the Germans continued firing back and showed no signs of giving up.

"Yo," Roy Lee shouted at the American group. "You guys don't look like Commandos. Must be pilots looking for a rendezvous. Need help?"

A voice came back with "What's the color of the day?"

I said, "Green, but if we were Germans, we could have just shot you instead of talking. How 'bout we move to your right flank and get closer to the open side of that wall, and maybe we can convince the Krauts to surrender."

"Okay, we'll take your help. When you get there fire a few rounds at that side of the church, so we know you're in place. Then we'll call for a surrender."

It worked and soon a white flag on the end of a German rifle appeared above the half-destroyed wall. An American pilot shouted *"hende kopf"* and the enemy put their hands on their heads. The pilots moved in cautiously, ordering more than a dozen Germans to their knees. We quickly retrieved their weapons and piled them on the wall next to us. A search of the other areas of the church discovered six other dead and wounded Germans and their weapons.

After a complete search of all the captives, we moved them to a large shell hole in the middle of the church. They were a ragged bunch. Half were teenage boys wearing shabby parts of German uniforms, homemade trousers, and mud-covered street shoes. The veteran German soldiers had various injuries, and many appeared near exhaustion. The pilots we helped insisted they needed to move on and asked if we'd hold the prisoners. "We'll send back the first medic we find."

Roy Lee and I decided to move into the corner of two surviving tall walls standing together in a ninety-degree angle that provided some protection from random enemy fire from the retreating Germans fleeing the British forces moving north from the Rhine River. We decided we could hold there in the church and take turns guarding the captives until a medic or British Commandos arrived.

We moved a broken section of a pew to one of the back walls. I sat down with Roy Lee and Jerry to contemplate how I got there in one piece and contemplate our next move. The remains of the church included some interconnecting walls, none higher than six or seven feet, with only a few roof rafters surviving over them.

This is not what I signed up for, and I worry how we're going to get back to base. For now, we're safe, and I know the war will be over in a few weeks, but at this moment, I've never felt more vulnerable.

Exiting the Waco glider (Silent Wings Museum)

11. VARSITY Volunteer in the Church

24 March, 1130 hours

OUR FEW minutes of peace was interrupted by a glank-glank-glank noise from behind the corner walls of the bombed-out church.

"That sounds like a tank," Roy Lee said, turning his head and eyes around the side wall. "Shit, it's a big one, a Tiger tank, followed by a half dozen troops coming up the hill about a half mile away. We better get out of here."

I turned to face the shell hole full of Germans. "What do we do with these guys? How do we leave this place, sneak out the back, in the open?"

Suddenly, we heard rustling sounds, movement coming from the cemetery through the large opening in the rear wall of the church.

"Did you hear that?" I said in a hushed voice. I placed a forefinger on my lips while looking at Roy Lee. He nodded. I motioned him to follow me. Staying low, we moved around the shell hole filled with prisoners to a door opening holding only the door frame. Peeking out at the old cemetery, I noticed movement among the weathered headstones.

Roy Lee leaned his head out the other side of the doorway. With a poor imitation of a native Brit, he said, "Fancy a cup 'o tea?"

The answer back was, "That all you got, is tea? Haven't you heard of Jim Beam?"

I replied, "Yeah, he's from Kentucky."

"Why didn't you say so? Good to know you're not Kraut or Brits," was the second reply from the cemetery.

A tall, slender American soldier with Sgt. stripes on his sleeve stepped from behind a large family marker named HELLER in the middle of many headstones. Four others appeared from other cemetery headstones. Two carried M-1 rifles, the Sgt. had a Thompson slung over his shoulder, and the fourth had what looked like an anti-tank gun, a bazooka.

Once again, a louder glank-glank-glank came from the other end of the church.

"Come in, Sergeant. Glad to see you. You hear that? I hope you can help us with that steel monster approaching," Roy Lee said.

"Yeah, and I see you have guests in church

today. Frankie has a bazooka, but if that's a Tiger tank, our big gun may only slow him down and make him more dangerous," the Sgt. said, eyeing the ragtag Germans in the shell hole.

"Follow me," Roy Lee said, and we led our small cavalry of troops around the prisoner-filled shell hole to the back corner of two rock walls.

Now grouped together and down on one knee, their leader with Sgt. stripes on his sleeve extended his hand to Roy Lee and introduced himself. "Doug Jenkins and my patrol, Frankie Simonelli, Jimmy DuPree, and Sal Amato."

We made self-introductions. "Lt. Roy Lee Harrison." He extended his hand. "This here is Lieutenant Bill McCallister, better known as Mac, and Flight Officer Jerry Griswold with the wounded wing."

"Good to see you, Sergeant," Jerry said and reached with his left hand.

"You showed up at an opportune time," I said. "Can you help us deal with that tank coming up the road?"

The Sgt. looked around the edge of the wall. "Damn. It is a Tiger. I'm thinking we need to flank him and his troops before he sees us. If we can pin down the troops, Frankie might be able to blow one of his tracks, disabling the Tiger from moving forward. These guys look like they're retreating from Monty's boys coming across the river. Let's move to their flank, get in closer, and then decide whether to engage or let them go by."

"Mac," Jerry said, "if you'll give me the burp gun, I'll stay here and guard our guests until you get back." I agreed after he explained that he wouldn't be much use since it was difficult for him to move quickly and he couldn't use a rifle while on the move. I handed him his burp gun I was carrying and promised we'd return. Jerry pointed the machine gun at the Germans in the shell hole, held his finger to his lips, and said, "SHHH."

Sgt. Jenkins led his men through a side opening, opposite the road. Roy Lee and I followed. We crawled over a stone fence into the trees surrounding the church yard. Moving slowly and quietly tree to tree, we made our way to within twenty yards of the tank patrol on their right flank. The huge tank continued, clank-clank-clank, slowly up the road toward the half-standing, gutted church. Six German infantry walked alongside and behind the big tank.

Jenkins waved up Frankie with his bazooka. Frankie knelt and readied the big gun on his shoulder. The tank stopped and rotated the turret to the church. Sal lifted a shell to load into the back of the gun when the German tank stopped rotating the big gun and fired…a thundering VROOMP, followed by an explosion at the corner of the two side walls standing together.

Grabbing our ears, we looked back at the old shell of a church and watched the familiar corner wall of the church explode, rocks, dirt, and debris spraying up and out in all directions.

"Damn," I blurted. "Why are they shooting?

That's where Jerry is guarding the German prisoners." I moved out from behind the tree with my Thompson pointing the way. I expected the Sgt. to order a charge or an attack signal and Frankie to fire the bazooka. One step more and I tripped over something hard at my ankles. I fell uncontrollably to the ground. After landing face first on wet leaves, I glanced back. Sgt. Jenkins tripped me.

"No, stop," he whispered, with a hand on my lower back. "Let 'em go. We can't help Jerry now, and we're outnumbered and outgunned."

"What?" I said. "We've got six guns and more fire power. Let's take 'em, and the bazooka will stop the tank. We can't abandon Jerry; he may still be alive and seriously hurt. You can still shoot the tank with the bazooka, stop it, and we'll take out the troops. Let's kill the bastards."

The Sgt. ordered Frankie to back off with the bazooka and waved our group to fall back instead of attacking the German tank patrol. Suddenly, my fear of war and face-to-face combat was replaced with rage. At that moment I wanted to attack and kill all German soldiers. I struggled for a moment against the Sgt.'s hold before his words began to make sense.

I outrank him but know he has more experience at maneuvers and three soldiers following his orders.

My body was shaking, the adrenaline rush about to explode inside me. Mixed feelings of fight-or-flight caused me to grit my teeth and bury my face in the leaves to hold back a scream.

Jenkins hand lightened. Still stunned, and mad,

I tried to lift my head and look around. Staying down, not moving, seemed a cowardly choice, and watching the tank blow up the church with Jerry inside also seemed cowardly. I felt a tap on my back and looked up to see Sgt. Jenkins's raised arm and hand pointing away from the road and German patrol.

I pushed up on all fours and heard him whisper, "Best we stay low. Let them move on to the church. We'll move to the west and find our people." His hand motioned to come, then his finger pressed to his lips. "Shh."

He moved off in a crouch away from the road, waving to the others to follow.

I followed with head and shoulders down. I couldn't erase my mind's image of the tank shot tearing Jerry to bits or crushing him under stone from the corner wall and wondering what happened to the German prisoners in the shell hole. Certainly, some of the wall stones rained down on them too. Could any have survived the tank shot?

Where are we going? I needed to check my map but I was too busy weaving through the trees, hoping the German patrol didn't hear us and take a shot at us. It was difficult leaving Griswold behind, not knowing if he was still alive.

Did he survive the tank shot? Probably not. I promised I'd go back for him. I had to keep moving with the Sgt. and our group. It was the better chance to survive the war. That rationalization didn't ease my conscience as we moved west through a damp, cold forest. The wet, mossy ground made it easy to walk quietly staying in the trees and underbrush and away from roads, which were full of retreating Germans.

After stepping through more than a mile of German forest as quietly as possible, Sgt. Jenkins held us at the edge of a wide clearing with a railroad track running through the middle. The Sgt. was on my right with his men on his right. I pulled out my map and located the railroad tracks in front of us.

We were northwest of our designated LZ-S and miles north of the Rhine. The rendezvous location was south at the intersection of a second railroad line that split off that line and moved in a northwest direction. A muddy ditch bordered the opposite side of the tracks.

I estimated it to be about fifty yards across the clearing and over the railroad to the next tree line. We knelt in a long line, starting with me, then Jenkins, who was pulling out his binoculars, his men lined up to his right, and Roy Lee on the far right. We quietly watched and listened for any movement across the clearing on the opposite tree line.

Jenkins turned to me. "I could tell you were upset at leaving the church after the tank blew out the walls left standing and likely killed Jerry. It's difficult for us to leave him but I thought it best to avoid the conflict. All the Krauts are in a retreat mindset. I say let 'em go."

"You're the infantry, Sergeant, so I deferred to you. I admit I've never been in ground combat. But in my judgment, we could have taken the bazooka shot to cripple the tank, killed the squad, and not left one of ours behind, dead or alive. Next time I may pull rank on you."

We studied the map showing the railroad track to our left turns southwest, and in the opposite direction it straightened out to the north of us then turned and appeared to run parallel to the Issel River. Sgt. Jenkins knelt beside a large tree and surveyed the opposite tree line with his binoculars. I heard a pop followed by a high-pitched zip then a swat that caused all of us to flinch.

Sgt. Jenkins released his binoculars and pitched forward into the open grass.

"Sniper, across the clearing in the trees," Corporal DuPree cried.

I reached for the Sgt.'s left leg and Jimmy reached over to Jenkins' right leg, and we pulled him back into the underbrush. The strap still around his neck brought the binoculars with him. Roy Lee picked up the binoculars, took off his flight cap, and went prone, scooting up in grass between the base of two trees. He scanned across the tree line on the other side of the tracks for the sniper.

We rolled Sgt. Jenkins over to see where he was hit. The bullet wound was through and through under his right collar bone. The impact knocked him out. He had a good pulse but was bleeding from both the entrance and outlet wounds.

Corporal Sal Amado had a first aid kit and was pulling out gauze and sulfa medication. "We've got to stop the bleeding," he exclaimed. "Let's prop his shoulder blade against the tree trunk and a gauze pack. That'll hold pressure on the wound, to slow down the bleeding."

By this time Sgt. Jenkins had come around. He reached for another gauze pack and held it tight under his field jacket.

Sal continued, "Sergeant Jenkins took the hit near his right shoulder, so I expect to see the shooter to our right. He must have fired from the trees at one or two o'clock and behind that clump of trees growing together. Let's see if we can flank him from both sides."

"Lieutenant, if you go left, I'll go right," said Amado. "One of us needs to get behind him or force him to expose himself trying to get a shot at one of us or run from our flanking maneuver."

"You want me to flank him?" I questioned. "I have a Thompson. I'd have to get within twenty yards to get a sure shot at him. He could pick me off before I get to the railroad track."

"You don't need to get close to him. Just move to your left like you are going to flank him," Sgt. Jenkins said.

Roy Lee said, "I'm on the right end. I'll run an end-around pattern. Who's going to take the shot?"

Sgt. Jenkins said, "Snipers are not as good at hitting a moving target. He might expose himself trying to aim at you or Roy Lee. Then Jimmy can take him out with his carbine."

"You get him to move and if I can get on him, he's a dead man," Jimmy said.

Roy Lee said, "If he takes a shot at the Lieutenant and you miss, Jimmy, I'll have a chance at him."

I thought, *Again, volunteered for a suicide mission.*

"Ready." Jimmy lifted his carbine to his shoulder. "One, two, three, GO."

I didn't step out in the clearing but turned left and stepped quickly behind the first row of trees. Moving in a crouch, I took only a few quick steps before falling on my face from something that ripped at my knees.

Damn, tripped again. This time it was a thorny vine tearing at my legs, then my hands and arms trying to break the fall. I heard a distant POP of a rifle, but the bullet didn't hit me or near me. I untangled from the vines and looked back to our original position. Another shot rang out, louder this time. Two more shots at the sniper came from Jimmy and Roy Lee.

"I think I hit him," Jimmy said. "But he's still moving." Blam, blam. He and Roy Lee fired again. "GO," Jimmy ordered. "Get to him before he can get reset. Frankie, are you hit?"

"No. Let's get him," Frankie said, and took several quick steps into the clearing in the sniper's direction. Sal Amato followed.

POP. Another shot. Sal stopped when he saw Frankie fall. Sal swung around to retreat. Then POP, the next shot hit Sal in the back.

Our assumption of one sniper was wrong. There are two.

"There must be another sniper," said Jimmy. "He got Frankie and Sal."

I ran back to the Sgt., glad to not be in pursuit of the snipers. The bleeding from his wound under his collarbone had slowed. He was awake. "Damn," he said.

He squinted and cringed before growling, "Help me up."

I gently held his shoulder down. "Best you stay still against that tree trunk to minimize the bleeding. Can Jimmy operate that bazooka if I load it?"

"Hell, yes; anyone can, even you. Just aim, hold tight, and pull the trigger."

"OK. Keep holding that gauze pack on the wound. Jimmy and I will try to take out the second sniper."

Jimmy reached for the bazooka. "Let's blow these Krauts away."

"Where are the shells?" I asked.

"In my backpack. I've got the bazooka. I'll kneel behind the big tree and aim from the right side. I know where the last shot came from. Let's do it."

Jimmy knelt behind the tree, and I loaded the shells. "See the darkest big tree with a stub of a dead branch sticking out the lower left side? He's on the ground under that tree stub," Jimmy said. "Lieutenant Harrison, if you'll give me some cover fire, get him to duck for a few seconds, I'll step out from behind this tree to get a clear shot at him."

"You got it buddy," Roy Lee replied.

"I'll move to the side of this tree and try to hit that tree he is hiding behind. I may not hit him but it could flush him out in the open so you can hit 'em or he'll run away."

The plan worked. Roy Lee sprayed some shots on the base of the tree and Jimmy leaned out and fired from the bazooka. The tree exploded and split down the middle with branches flying in all directions. The sniper crawled out of the shower of tree limbs and twigs, jumped up, and tried to run in the opposite direction, but fell on his face and didn't move.

Assuming we're safe for a few minutes, we turned our attention to Frankie, who hadn't moved from where he fell, and Sal, who was semi-conscious and groaning.

Roy Lee dropped the bazooka, grabbed his Thompson machine gun and ran toward the downed enemy snipers. I followed him, sprinting across the road and tracks. We found both snipers dead.

We returned to where Frankie and Sal were hit. Frankie was gone, hit squarely in the chest, probably died instantly.

The second sniper hit Sal in his lower back and the bullet was still inside him. He was losing a lot of blood and we couldn't determine how bad he was hurt internally. The shot probably did some serious internal damage because it was difficult to stop the bleeding. We dumped in sulfa and used gauze packs with pressure on the entrance wound to slow the hemorrhage, but he was in agony. In less than two minutes, he expired.

12. Escape from the Church

24 March, 1140 hours

JERRY LISTENED for any sounds of Mac, Roy Lee, and Jenkins' group attacking the tank and German patrol. He could still hear the glank-glank movement of the tank but nothing else. No gunshots. He realized they hadn't attacked the German squad.

He thought, *Maybe Mac and the Sgt.'s group have moved on. I'm not staying here. Those German troops will be on us in a minute. I'm getting out of here.* With his right arm still wrapped in gauze in a sling around his neck, he picked up the burp gun with his left and headed for the opening in the half-wall on the other side of the shell hole.

He walked casually around the shell hole with

eyes on the prisoners to let them know he was still watching them. Most of the glances were casual and no effort was made to move nor question where he was going. None rose to resist or follow. When he passed through a large opening in the wall and out of sight of the Germans, he looped burp gun belt over his head with the gun hanging on his back. He quietly picked up his pace into the weed-overgrown cemetery, weaving around headstones. He knew he needed to move out of the area as fast as he could before the tank and German squad arrived.

His thoughts were racing. *I don't know which direction our guys went. Mac, or the Sgt., must have decided the Germans were too many and avoided them. I guess I don't blame them, except Mac said he would be back and I didn't expect him to leave without me.*

BOOM! An explosion behind him sent stones and debris into the whole area. A shock wave followed, shaking the remaining church structure and trees around it. The shock wave from the big gun pushed him forward, causing him to trip over a marker in the cemetery. He tried to stop his fall by extending his left hand to a tall headstone. The hand and arm caught the edge of the upright slab, turning him around so that he fell backward to the ground. He felt his head hit hard before blacking out.

The blackout was unlike anything he'd ever experienced before. He felt his body floating above the ground and an ecstatic emotion taking his mind into the clouds. For a few moments he had a climactic feeling of calm joy like he'd never known. Totally relaxed, in the absence of any pain. He was in a dream state and his subconscious thought was, *I don't know what this is, but I'm enjoying it for however long it lasts.*

The tank moved forward to the damage it created, the German troops surrounding the church rubble. There were cries from under the rubble and the German squad moved quickly to help, discovering the cries were coming from German soldiers buried under the rubble resulting from the German tank's shot. Some were dead, others badly wounded, and only two were able to walk.

In the meantime, an American patrol of glider troops heard the tank shot plus explosion and took cover on both sides of a curve in the road not knowing what they were about to encounter ahead. Their leaders were a Lt. English and Maj. Maxwell. The officers decided to send a two-man patrol to do a reconnaissance of the shot and explosion and report back.

The two-man patrol reached the church scene as the tank squad was pulling out the injured German soldiers from the shell hole inside the half-destroyed church walls. They noticed the injured German soldiers being helped had no weapons and there was nothing to explain why a German a Tiger tank and squad would have fired on their own unarmed soldiers.

The squad leader, without a medic, ordered his men to use whatever first aid they had to patch up the ones with minor injuries. Some of the more severely injured were loaded onto the tank. Some couldn't be moved and were given pain medication before the tank and squad moved on. There was no sign that American or British troops were involved. The American two-man recon team quickly returned to their troops to report what they saw.

"Major Maxwell and Lieutenant, we think the shot we heard was a German tank firing into a partially demolished church, hitting their own troops. We don't think they could see or knew ahead of time there were German soldiers in the church, and we could see no evidence of Allied troops being engaged. The tank squad helped patch up a couple of the injured that could walk, took some of the more severely wounded on the tank, and left the dead and severely wounded in the rubble."

"How many German soldiers in the squad?" the corporal asked.

"Six, with only Mauser rifles. No anti-tank weapons or automatic guns."

They began to hear the glank-glank sound of the tank as it approached on the road near the curve.

"Let's stay down and let this group pass," said Lt. English. "We don't have an anti-tank gun, and they're bound to encounter the British Commandos coming this way in the next hour or so. Commandos have the firepower to defeat this small group."

Within minutes the German tank and squad passed the Americans without contact.

The Lt. and Maj. discussed the next move. "I think we need to examine the site to determine if any Allied soldiers were involved before we move on."

"All right, men, let's move out quietly up to the church rubble," the Lt. said. "We want to survey the area for details of what happened and whether any Allied soldiers were involved or injured. It's difficult to believe the Germans just accidentally fired on their own troops without Allied troops being involved. If they had no arms, maybe American troop riders like us captured them earlier and disarmed them before the tank squad arrived."

Rounding the curve in the road in the opposite direction, they saw the church rubble with dying and dead Germans still in what was left. The American squad had a medic, and he attended to those who were still alive.

"All right men," the Maj. said. "Let's all spread out and around the area to find any clue as to others involved in this skirmish. There may be dead or injured Americans or British in the area. The troop riders and officers, two pilots, and five soldiers spread out to find any further evidence of a previous fight."

The Maj. rode a C-47 troop carrier in the assault wave. He bailed out when anti-aircraft fire hit them hard, and this squad of glider troops discovered him unhurt on the ground.

Maj. Maxwell walked off the road and around the partial west wall, the only wall left standing. Ahead of him a corporal was walking into the overgrown graveyard, almost tripping over headstones.

"Whoa. Major," the corporal shouted. "Over here. I think I've found one of ours."

The Maj. stepped carefully toward the corporal. He had found an American, but he was either unconscious or dead and not dressed in infantry clothing. The Maj. arrived and bent to check the pulse of the man, who the Maj. easily recognized as a glider pilot and said so to the corporal when he stepped up.

"He's one of our glider pilots and is alive but with a weak pulse. Doesn't appear to have been shot but somehow knocked unconscious." The corporal picked up Jerry's burp machine gun and looked it over.

"This burp gun doesn't look like it's been fired, Major He has a head wound that needs attention. Probably suffered a concussion falling on one of these stones. His arm is loosely bandaged and looks like multiple hits and cuts. Maybe shrapnel wounds from exploding flak while in the air."

"Medic. Over here," the corporal shouted with a wave of his hand.

The medic arrived and checked Jerry's heart and pupil response. He popped open smelling salts that brought him around, still groggy and disoriented.

"What happened? Where am I?" he mumbled.

The medic said, "You have suffered a concussion. Are you hurt anywhere else? I don't see any other major injury. Lie still and let me redress this arm. Are you a glider pilot? What's your name?"

"Yes, I'm Flight Officer Jerry Griswold. We got hit by an AA gun just as we were about out to land. That's what tore up my arm. My copilot was Lieutenant McCallister." He went on to describe how they got there and who was in the group. "I'm a little hazy about what has happened since. We were guarding some Germans we captured when the church was shelled. Don't remember any more until you found me. My head hurts like hell."

"I'm thinking you were leaving the church rubble, and you tripped and fell hitting your head on a stone marker. And I guess you don't know where the rest of your group is," the medic asked.

"No, sorry. Don't know where they went," Jerry said.

"OK. Rest here a few minutes. Don't try to stand. I think we'll move on soon and you can go with us if you're able," said the medic, who continued to clean and re-bandage Jerry's badly injured right arm.

The Maj. pulled out one of the assault maps. "Lieutenant, this road should intersect with a north–south main road that we can take north into the other landing and drop zones. There should be pilot rendezvous area and aid station set up by now in these zones. Leave a couple of your troops with the medic to assist and the rest of us will move on. We may be able find someone with a jeep or truck to come back for them."

13. Mueller Farm

24 March, 1200 hours

WHEN HANS and Otto arrived at the Mueller farm, they stopped at the water well near the back door, took a big gulp of water, and filled their canteens. They entered through the back door into the kitchen. Hans turned into a utility room, then through a door, down a steep stairway, and into the cellar. From heavy-duty wooden shelves stacked against an earthen wall, Hans pulled out two bottles of wine from his special collection.

Back up in the kitchen, Otto selected a drip coffee pot, added water, and lit the gas stove to brew coffee. With fresh coffee and an open bottle of

Bordeaux, the two old farmers sat at the chrome and melamine kitchen table and relaxed for a few minutes, feeling back at home.

"You got anything left in that barn, Hans?" Otto said, looking out the kitchen window.

"Not much. Animals are all gone. Only a rusting tractor that hasn't run for over a year. I had some pigs and cows. Sold the pigs when Hitler invaded Poland. Later the *Heer*, army, came in and took the remaining livestock to feed the troops. Made no payment, just confiscated my animals. That's when I sent my wife and daughter to England to stay with a cousin. Come, let me show you some changes to the barn before the other soldiers get here. Like yours, built by my father and grandfather, only bigger and last fall I worked to enlarge the room below the upper floor and added a special space."

They went out the back door headed for the huge red Mueller barn, taller than the two-story farmhouse. Hans stopped to proudly explain the construction. "As you know the foundation is stone, with a strong floor made up of heavy beams and wood planks. The earth was pushed up against the foundation to the level of the floor for access to the main floor. There are only three sides to the foundation, leaving one side open to store the tractor and other implements underneath the floor.

"Yes, I know" Otto said. "I've always envied the construction, wish my barn had been built in the same way. Mine is big enough but sits on a simple rock foundation with no basement underneath.

Hans continued. "Yes, that's where we store tools, feed, fertilizer, and other stuff for protection from the weather. The opening underneath at the side with no foundation faces south, again away from winter storms from the north."

Hans waved him to follow. "Come, I want to show you something important." He went to the lower level, which was protected by two large gates hinged like doors that opened to the large space under the barn. Hans opened one gate to show the rusting tractor and other implements and storage items.

He led Otto to the back wall made of vertical wood planks. Butted up against both side walls were shelves on one side and a feeding trough on the other. In the center of the wall, Hans stepped on a board ledge, giving him enough height to reach an iron ring near the top of the wide wood planks nailed together and pulled out a linchpin releasing the plank wall, which fell to the dirt floor. Behind it was a smaller door cut into the stone foundation. He reached for a handle-latch and swung it open.

"This is our cellar we use to store food, fruit in jars, wine, canned goods and guns and ammunition. The barrels are full of water for emergencies. If I don't make it when the war is over, you get over here and get this stuff before the Nazis or Russians, or even the Americans, find it."

"That's very kind of you, Hans. Both of us may need this before this war is over."

Hans and Otto were about to return to the house when they heard what sounded like a truck or military vehicle approaching. Hans pushed up the plank wall. "Close the gates." Otto pulled the gates closed. Through open spaces in the gate, they watched a German patrol of six soldiers and an officer arrive in a half-track personnel vehicle. It had a mounted machine gun behind the front seats. The two men riding in back unloaded another machine gun and moved into the farmhouse. One of the soldiers returned to the half-track and drove it across the front yard, around to the side of the house.

"Otto, I don't want to go back in the house. I don't think we want to get involved with those troops. They're here to stop the Allied armies from moving up this road to destroy the bridges on the Issel River. They probably expect we've come and gone. They'll be happy to find the wine. Let's just lay low for now."

"I agree, Hans. But how long can we hide here? If we are found later, they might decide we are traitors and shoot us."

"Yes, Otto, but if they head this way we can go back into the cellar and pull up the wall to cover us. For now, let's wait and see what happens next."

They watched the German soldiers set up machine gun positions in a first-floor window and in an upstairs window. The others, including an officer, could be seen going into the kitchen and finding the wine Hans left on the table.

In less than an hour Hans and Otto saw a similar squad of soldiers. This time they looked like British, moving up the road to the farmhouse. Again, they counted six men and one or two officers. When they were almost directly in front of the house, the Germans opened fire, immediately killing two soldiers and scattering the others, who took cover in the trees across the road and to the south side of the house. The British returned fire but had little chance of hitting the Germans behind the windows upstairs and down. Hans and Otto couldn't see the front of the house but could hear the machine gun firing at the British in the trees across the road from the front of the house.

The farmers watched the two British soldiers in cover a few yards from the side of the house move toward the back corner. Then they heard a big gun fire from across the road, followed by an explosion from the front of the house. The two soldiers at the side of the house used that explosion as a diversion and rushed the shooters firing from the windows. Each pulled the pin on a grenade and tossed them into a window.

The grenade explosions silenced the last German guns. The British moved to the house from across the road. It appeared a German officer and one young soldier came out, surrendering, waving a white shirt. The British marched them back to their vehicle and on up the road toward the Issel River.

Hans and Otto left the barn and walked quietly into the farmhouse to check for survivors. There were none.

They were about to settle in the kitchen again when Hans said, "Let's pick up a couple of these soldier's guns and ammo. Much more fire power plus a shotgun, and we will probably need 'em before the day's over." Otto found an MP40 *Maschinenpistole* automatic pistol, and Hans picked up a bolt-action sniper rifle. The MP40 pistol had just one magazine with a half dozen rounds. The rifle had only three shots left in the clip.

"Now we can defend against the British, the Americans, and maybe the Wehrmacht, if necessary," Hans said.

German barn

14. Sgt. Bolton's Jeep

24 March, 1130 hours

THE TROOP riders from Griswold and McCallister's glider had orders to help secure a bridge over the Issel River north of LZS. They were to join up with troops from the British 2nd Battalion. Sgt. Bolton was riding in the jeep driven by Corporal Vincent with a 30-caliber machine gun and three additional glider-rider troops following on foot. Bolton and his squad moved north on a well-traveled road their map showed leading to an Issel River bridge.

Coming upon the top of a hill, Bolton's squad heard shots fired up ahead, followed by sounds of machine gun fire and several more POP, POPs from small arms. The jeep and squad moved to the top of the next rise and off the road out of sight. A half mile away at the low point in the road there was a large two-story farmhouse with a red barn in the back. A machine gun was firing from a second-story window and rifle fire came from windows on the left side. Moving slowly through the trees the squad began a circular move around the farmhouse.

They halted again within a hundred yards at an angle off the corner of the house and level with the eve of the roof. Sgt. Bolton pulled up his binoculars, surveyed the troops firing back, and recognized their British uniforms. They could be members of the Second Battalion of British Commandos, whom Bolton's men were supposed to help secure bridge six at the Issel River.

Bolton and his squad were discussing how they could help when one of the Second Battalion soldiers behind a tree fifty yards from the front of the farmhouse fired what sounded like an anti-tank gun, or a M40 recoilless rifle. The shot blew the big wooden front doors off their hinges. Two other paratroopers used the distraction of the door explosion to rush the side of the house and toss a grenade into a second-floor window and another into the first-floor window.

The exploding grenades quieted the machine gun upstairs and drove several enemy soldiers out the wide-open front door waving a white flag. Two of the enemy came out, an officer and young soldier, a small young man, maybe in his teens, wearing a shabby uniform too large for him, and another heavyset old man in farmer's clothes. Typical dress of the German army in these final weeks of the war.

"OK, men. They don't need our help," Bolton said. "Let's move on to the river."

They proceeded through the trees parallel to the road, and when they reached a flat open area, they heard more machine gun fire and saw black smoke rising above the trees in front of them. Continuing forward through the trees they saw the wreckage of a C-47 with a pretty girl in a red swimsuit, Georgia Gal, painted on her nose.

"Isn't that our tow plane from A-58?" Bolton asked.

"Yes, I think so," Brownie answered. "They got hit hard after cutting us loose. I thought they wouldn't survive. Looks like a great piece of flying to survive a belly landing along that tree line. The machine gun was raking the fuselage of the C-47 laying on its belly. Sounds much like the German version of our thirty-caliber Browning."

Sgt. Bolton tossed a canvas bag to Corporal Smith. "Corporal, you and the men take this first aid kit down to that aircraft crew that probably suffered serious injuries. Stay low, quiet, and out of sight of the Krauts firing that machine gun. Brownie and I are going to flank that gun and take it out."

Brownie drove the jeep slowly and quietly around the tall trees to within fifty yards behind the German machine gun emplacement. He saw two soldiers firing a tripod-mounted machine gun sitting behind a fallen tree trunk. Brownie put the jeep into position for a line-of-sight shot at the Germans and set the jeep brake.

Sgt. Bolton stood up at the jeep's 30-caliber gun, aimed, and fired off a burst of ten shots. The first few rounds ricocheted off the ground to one side of the gun and the next burst destroyed the gun and hit both Germans.

Corporal Brown put the jeep in gear and drove up to what was left of the gun and German soldiers.

"Check them out," Sgt. Bolton said, still aiming the jeep's gun at the German still-moving survivor. The corporal said one was dead and the other was still alive.

"He's got a pulse, Sarge, but he was hit at least three times and losing a lot of blood."

"All right, we can't save him. Let's move down to the C-47 wreck and see if they need more help." Corporal Brown got back in the jeep and they moved slowly to the wrecked C-47.

Bud and his crew looked back up the hill when they heard a second machine gun and watched Bolton and his jeep gun take out the German machine gun. Momentarily Corporal Smith and two men arrived with the first aid kit. Bud and his crew were still cheering.

"Boy, are we glad to see you all," Bud said. "They had us pinned down tight. I don't think we could have survived much longer. Was it just a single machine gun or did you see other Germans?"

"We only saw the one machine gun firing at you, no other infantry nearby," the corporal answered.

"They may have bugged out some time ago. Here's more medical supplies you might need."

Sgt. Bolton and Brownie arrived in the jeep and introduced themselves and the other men.

"Your Georgia Gal pulled us all the way from airfield A-58," Sgt. Bolton said. "Thanks for the bumpy, and sickly, but safe trip. Looks like Georgia Gal took some big hits. I'd say you did some outstanding flying to survive the belly landing."

"Well, thanks, but not all of us made it," Bud answered. "We lost our radio operator, Sergent Campbell, to the same anti-aircraft fire that knocked us down. We have some others injured. Can you direct us to a friendly aid station?"

"Wish I could, Lieutenant I'm guessing your best bet is to go back to the road west of here, then south on the road. I expect there will be one before you get to Wesel. We just saw some troopers from Monty's Second Battalion clean the enemy out of a big farmhouse about a half mile down the road, so you should not run into any Krauts."

"Great, thanks. I guess you men are headed for the bridges up on the Issel River?"

"Yeah, we're supposed to help that same British Second Battalion hold the number six bridge another mile up this road," Bolton answered. "Anything else we might help you with, Lieutenant?"

"No, but we could use some transportation. Us flyboys are untrained for walking very far. Our radio is still operational, and Lieutenant Hunt is on it trying raise someone to get us some help and directions to the nearest aide station. We'll stay put until we locate a safer place. Plan B might be moving toward the road and that farmhouse you guys cleared out. May be a good place to hold up until we get a ride to an aide station. Thanks, much, for your help. We were sittin' ducks for that machine gun. Good luck to you all."

The Bolton's squad moved out toward the road that leads north to the Issel River. Lt. Hunt wasn't getting anyone on the radio and turned to check their map.

"Bud, the map shows there's a planned aide station just north of Wesel on the road Bolton's squad took north. It's about a half mile west to that road and that farm may be where we can lay low and maybe get a ride down to Wesel or the aide station."

"Agree," said Bud. "We could be three-plus kilometers from the edge of town. Too far for this wounded group to travel. We might be able to make it but would be exposed to any Kraut patrol or retreating group. Let's move closer to the road and find that farm Sergeant Bolton talked about. If the Brits cleaned out the enemy, we can hold up in it until we find help."

The group moved slowly in the direction Bolton indicated to find the farmhouse and road to Wesel. Bud was hurting but able to move slowly. Lt. Legs Hunt was point man for the group, seeking the easiest route. They had bandaged and splinted Lt. Coffman's injured leg and he leaned on a makeshift crutch that allowed him to limp forward. After twenty minutes of slow trekking, they saw the farmhouse in the distance, recognizing the blown-off front door and a partially blown-out second-story wall. They also saw the barn in the rear.

"We don't want to occupy that house. It's too vulnerable, too wide open. I think we'd be smarter to hide in the barn," Lt. Hunt said.

"I agree," Bud said. "Why don't we go down to the tree line that fronts the road. Hunt and I will do a recon on the house. If it's quiet and as uninhabited as it looks, we'll signal you and Coffman to come on and we'll all go to the barn."

15. Bud Sullivan's Crew to the Meuller Farm

1330 hours

BUD AND Legs Hunt moved quietly, trying to stay in cover as they approached the farmhouse. Coffman, with a painful leg injury, held back in the trees. When the two reached the road, they saw the damage done by the bazooka to the front door, and the windows on one side were blown out. It was doubtful any Krauts were still alive or holed up waiting to ambush the Americans. Seeing no sign of life, they started across the road toward the front of the house.

In the kitchen Hans and Otto were finishing the few remnants of wine the Germans left when Otto spotted the Americans coming across the road.

"Hans. Look, someone is coming. I see two soldiers, look like Americans, coming toward the house."

"Come on, Otto. Let's get back to the barn. Maybe when they see all these dead Germans, they'll leave."

They moved quickly and quietly out the kitchen door, headed to the barn, and kept the house between them and the barn. They went straight back, circling the barn and moving around to the barn's lower gates.

Meanwhile, Bud and Lt. Hunt were entering the front of the house. The doors were blown to splinters by the British and several dead Germans lay inside. Lt. Hunt walked and crawled carefully up the damaged stairs to discover more dead Germans and a machine gun.

"Wow," Lt. Hunt said. "The Brits did a number on this bunch. I'm guessing this German squad was trying to keep the Brits from going up to the bridges at Issel." He came down the stairs just as carefully and followed Bud Sullivan down a short hall to the kitchen.

"I see somebody enjoyed a wine party here in the kitchen," Bud observed. "Notice there are few weapons around. Some German or Allied scavengers have picked up their weapons and ammo. We need to check out that barn. First, let's signal Coffman to come on down."

Coffman hobbled across the road and through what was left of the front door. The three men went through the kitchen and out the back door toward the barn.

Hans and Otto watched the two Americans searching the farmhouse and heard talk about going to the barn. The Americans walked up the incline to the doors on the upper side and slowly, carefully, with weapons ready, opened the barn doors on the upper level.

Hans heard them walking around on the floor above and gestured to his friend. "Otto, come over to this side of the tractor. We can hide till they come in down here," he whispered. "We'll capture them and wait for the others of our Volkssturm." Otto moved around the tractor and backed against the wall next to Hans.

Finding nothing in the upper level of the barn, the three airmen walked out and down to the back gates at the lower level.

Lt. Hunt peaked in through the slats in the back gate. All he saw was the old rusting tractor, an empty large room, and a large opening in the back wall. There was no lock on the gate latch, so he pulled hard on it until it started to open, dragging the front corner in the dirt.

Bud pulled a slat in the gate and together they pulled the gate wide open. They crept in, weapons at the ready, walking slowly along the side of the tractor with eyes on the opening of the back wall. When they reached the front of the tractor, in the center of the room, two men stepped out.

Hans said loudly, "Halt."

Otto moved around the rear of the tractor, behind the two Americans, and said, "Hands up, or we shoot! Guns down."

The airmen knew they were caught and surrendered, laying their guns on the dirt floor.

"Pistol, too," Hans said.

Lt. Hunt had a .45 automatic he lifted slowly from its holster and set next to his Thompson machine gun.

Hans said, "Move," pointing to the back wall. "Down."

Otto picked up the weapons and placed them on the front wall corner near where they'd previously hidden.

Hans stepped from the side with a German machine gun pointed at Sullivan. "Hands up," he said loudly. "Guns down," pointing for him to move over with the others.

Hans tried to explain in broken English their hatred of Hitler and the farmer's sympathy for the Americans. "We are not going to shoot you, but we can't let you go not knowing what will happen to us. We are hoping the Allies will defeat Hitler soon and maybe we will get our farms back. That's all we want. To be farmers again, not soldiers, not killers."

Otto nodded in agreement.

"Where are your farms?" Bud asked.

"This is my farm," Hans said. "Otto's farm is next to mine on north side. We convinced the Volkssturm captain we could help hold this location on the road and stop the Allies from moving north to capture the bridge over the Issel River. We hid in here while the British defeated a squad of German soldiers who took over my farmhouse and tried to stop the British from moving up the road north to the river. We do not want to fight the Americans and British. We just want to save our farms. Eventually, the Nazis are going to surrender, Hitler killed or captured. We hope the Communist don't take over Germany when that happens."

16. McCallister Pilots and Troops

24 March, 1400 hours

I SURVIVED the sniper attack, and Lt. Roy Lee Harrison wasn't hurt, but we lost two good men. Jimmy DuPree helped a severely injured Sgt. Jenkins when our group moved across the railroad tracks headed for a road the map showed linking the town of Wesel to the bridges over the Issel River. According to the army map, it was southwest about a mile away.

Roy Lee and I knew Sgt. Jenkins was in trouble. His wound was still bleeding through the bandaging of his upper chest and back. He needed medical help soon or he'd bleed out and die if we moved him anymore.

Lt. Harrison also helped Sgt. Jenkins, but both DuPree and Harrison were exhausted and not able to go much further.

We've got to find the road and go south to find the designated aide station at the edge of the town of Wesel. The wounded are still bleeding, getting weaker from loss of blood. I don't think we're strong enough to reach the road to Wesel.

We'd traveled only a kilometer when Roy Lee fell to the ground trying to hold Sgt. Jenkins up. They were both on their knees. We all struggled and crawled over against a farm stone wall to rest and check on Jenkins' condition. If we kept going, he could bleed to death. We were out of bandages and had no morphine for the pain.

"Roy Lee, I think you should rest here with Jenkins, stay quiet and continue to keep pressure on his would, trying to stop or reduce his loss of blood. Jimmy and I will go on to find the road that goes south to where the map said there should be an aide station. We'll see if we can find help there and we'll come be back with a medic as soon as possible. Come on Jimmy, follow me and stay low behind this wall."

We reached a corner where another wall connects and looked over to see a rutted, winding, dirt road turning southeast around a curve. "This road turns west and may connect to the main road to Wesel we're looking for. Let's pick up the pace and follow the road. You walk on the left side; I'll follow the ditch on the right."

In less than a hundred yards we came to a

creek running through a concrete culvert under the road. After hopping the creek, Jimmy turned and whispered across the dirt road, "Shh, hear that? Somebody is coming, behind us. Take cover." We both backed away from the dirt road.

The faint noise sounded like a wheel rolling along the road, but there was no other sound. When we looked back, we saw a man in a German uniform with his head and shoulders down peddling a bicycle hard and fast directly at us.

What's he running from or to? Is he trying to rejoin a larger group? I think I'll stop him.

I stepped onto the road as the young German approached with his head down and eyes on the road. "Halt, halt," I said loudly, holding my Thompson waist high and pointed in his direction to let the German know I was serious.

The German looked up at me with a wide-eyed, shocked expression. He hit his brakes, causing the bike to skid in the dirt and gravel, then made a sharp turn to his right, off the road, to avoid hitting me. He bumped over the shallow ditch, tried to peddle again, and wobbled through the field for a few yards before the front wheel hit something hard and threw him over the handlebars to the ground.

My mind was still trying to figure out what this guy could be doing. Where was he going?

I thought, *How strange, a lone soldier on a bicycle in uniform but without a helmet or rifle.*

I watched, standing frozen; he wasn't much of a threat. I was still wondering what he was about when the young German struggled to his feet. I walked across the shallow ditch continuing to hold my Thompson on him.

I saw he had a sidearm in a holster hanging from his belt on his left side but turned backward. He tried to avoid us, yet he was the enemy and may have been working with those snipers that shot Sergeant Jenkins or Frankie. I watched without moving and he did the same as our eyes connected.

His right hand moved across his body toward the sidearm.

How is he going to pull out that pistol turned backwards on his left side?

The sudden sound of gunfire interrupted my thought and the recoil from my Thompson machine gun brought me to my senses. Even though I hadn't consciously decided to shoot him, it was as if the gun knew I had to shoot him. A double shot from the Thompson hit him in the chest. He fell flat on his back on the ground next to the bike.

Then I was the one in shock. *I have never shot anyone. What do I do now?*

I slowly walked over to him, and Jimmy came running. I had several encounters with the enemy today. None required a face-to-face conflict. At times I'd been sick at my stomach thinking of what I would do when faced with a kill-or-be-killed confrontation. It happened, but not like I ever imagined. I didn't feel strong, or brave or in any way satisfied, only sad it happened. He wasn't an immediate threat to me; and yet, he was about to be, if I hadn't reacted as I did.

When do you consciously decide to shoot? When is it the right time to kill somebody, even the enemy?

Jimmy knelt next to the young soldier and touched his neck, feeling for the carotid artery and a pulse. "Good shot," Jimmy said and shook his head side to side. "Looks like he's done for. One of those shots in his chest got his heart. Died instantly."

"C'mon, let's get out of here," I said. We hurried down the dirt road. Within minutes we arrived at the intersection of the main road, left to Wesel and right or north to the Issel River.

"Let's hold up here and watch what moves on this road, friend or foe." In the distance I heard heavy artillery and small arms fire from the north. We decided to move south toward Wesel and picked up the pace. The map showed that we were a mile or less from where the expected aide station should be.

"Let's move over to the other side of the road. There's more cover in case we encounter Krauts."

We double-timed down the side of the road and luckily didn't encounter the enemy. After almost a mile we came over a hill and there before us was the rubble that had been Wesel. A large bivouac tent was set at the side of the road with jeeps, medics, and what looked like doctors scurrying about. We broke into a jog, eventually running by a group at a table in front of a tent with a large red cross painted on it.

A man in a white coat grabbed us as we attempted to enter the tent. "Whoa, there, gentlemen, this is an operating area. You can't come in here. See the Lieutenant and nurse at the check-in table out front." Since the man had a white operating cap on his head and captain's bars on his collar, we quickly turned and exited through the tent flap we'd come in.

At the check-in table we found a Lt. and two medics unloading a stretcher with a patient off the hood. "Sir, we need help with two wounded men we left behind about three kilometers up the road. Is there any way we can get a medic and jeep to go back and get them?"

He pointed to the same jeep. "There's a jeep if you can get the soldier who drove it to help you." A medic returned from the operating tent and got back in his jeep.

I stopped him and described our situation. At first, he said he couldn't go, his responsibility was to his company. When I explained that the pickup of our wounded wasn't far away and we could be back in less than an hour, he finally agreed. In moments, we loaded the stretcher on the hood of the jeep and headed back up the road.

Roy Lee and Jenkins had moved into a grove of trees, and I could tell they were in bad shape. All the blood lost was taking a toll. Sgt. Jenkins was loaded onto the stretcher and the medic gave him a shot of morphine. He helped Roy Lee into the right seat.

Jimmy and I were about to climb in the back when rifle fire came at us from up the road. We hit the ground and returned fire toward incoming but couldn't see the enemy firing at us. The medic gunned the engine, wheeled the jeep around, and accelerated down the dirt road back toward the aide station.

17. Surrounded on the Dirt Road

24 March 1430 hours

S UDDENLY, Corporal Jimmy DuPree and I were taking fire from two directions. We rolled into the shallow roadside ditch but had no idea where the shots were coming from. We were exposed and very vulnerable. They could have walked up to us and killed us. It was just a matter of time before they picked us off.

"Let's give it up, Jimmy. We're dead if we try to return fire or run. There's little or no cover nearby. We're told they don't take prisoners, but we're dead staying here. The only chance may be to surrender and hope for an opportunity to escape."

"I agree. I'm with you, Lieutenant McCallister,"

Jimmy said, and raised his rifle above his head. I did the same.

Four Germans moved in and grabbed my Thompson and DuPree's carbine. One of the Germans was an officer; I guessed by his cap and shoulder boards he was a captain, and his collar displayed the lightning bolts of the "SS" or Gestapo, Waffen-SS. His driver, also an SS, drove onto the dirt road in the German equivalent of a jeep, called a *Kubelwagen*. It had a larger passenger area than a jeep with a full backseat.

One of the Germans approached us and took my side arm, a .45 automatic strapped across my shoulder and chest. He then pointed to move down the road ahead of the *Kubelwagen* with hands in the air. The soldiers jumped in the *Kubelwagen* driven by a young soldier not over twenty-one, pushing us toward the main road to Wesel. The officer barked orders in German and the only word I understood was *Bauernhaus*.

I said to Jimmy quietly, "I think he said 'farmhouse' in German. They're taking us to a farmhouse. Probably to shoot us there. Must be a location they know the Germans still hold."

When we reached the main road, we were ordered to turn right and move faster. We walked fast and kept it up for ten to twenty minutes, then saw a farmhouse a hundred yards ahead. It was heavily damaged from a previous skirmish.

I wondered if we were going to see injured or dead Americans. More likely the latter since we knew there was an order from Hitler to take no prisoners. I guessed we were still alive for a reason. Maybe for trading purposes. As we got closer, I noticed there was no sign of movement, and no guards outside. The place was nearly destroyed, and no one was visible in or around the farmhouse.

The German officer called, "Halt" as we reached the side yard of the farmhouse. Two of the soldiers got out of the vehicle and it continued to the front of the damaged farmhouse. The officer and driver trudged inside to survey the damage and see if there were Germans in control. It was obvious the battle was recent, with freshly splintered wood and broken stone.

The soldiers guarding us were clearly not veterans. In fact, one was young, possibly a recent recruit, just old enough to legally drink, but in full infantry uniform. The other, much older, could have been part of the home guard, not dressed as regular infantry. The officer and his driver returned with angry looks.

It was quiet during their visit inside the farmhouse, which implied no active soldiers were inside. What they saw inside was dead Germans. Not what these Germans expected; this was not the German outpost they expected. The two got back into the *Kubelwagen* and ordered us to move ahead of them as they turned toward the barn. When we reached the lower opened gate to the barn, another older German, big with arms and hands like a farmer or one of the home guard men escorting us, walked out to greet us.

"Herr Captain. Welcome. Come, we have more prisoners inside. I will take these men you have and put them with the others."

"Who are you and why are you here?" the German captain said. "We have orders from Der Führer that all prisoners will be shot."

"I am Hans Mueller. My comrade Otto and I are Volkssturm soldiers assigned to this post to halt our enemy from proceeding up this road to the bridges over the Issel River. We stopped and captured these men just an hour or so ago," he said, pointing to the American airmen standing against the back wall of the barn.

"We must execute them and the ones we captured," exclaimed the young German driver. Then he grabbed Jimmy by the arm, shoved him toward the back wall and said in broken English, "Line up with enemies. We shoot all."

The German officer pointed for me to move forward over to the other American prisoners.

"Over against the wall with the others," the German captain said.

As Jimmy and I walked toward the American prisoners, I immediately recognized my friend "Bud" Sullivan.

Where the hell did he come from? Why the hell is he here? How in the world, at the end of this crazy day, did we arrive together in the same place?

I wanted to tell him I hadn't forgotten his gift to me that morning. He smiled back discretely, trying not to look surprised and raise additional attention.

Since my back was to our captors, I smiled and raised my eyebrows in a surprise greeting. I wanted to tell him I was fully capable of using what he gave me, but I was a little nervous about the timing, when and how.

Just be calm and wait for the right opportunity. Then do it without hesitation.

The captain's driver walked in next to him and turned to motion for the other Germans guards to come in. The prisoners were all together against the wall. Pvt. Jimmy DuPree and I moved to the left of Bud Sullivan and the other two Americans on his right. The two old Germans who were already in the barn with Bud stood to one side.

The young German driver abruptly said, "Now we shoot them. We are not keeping any prisoners."

"No. It is not necessary to kill these men," said one of the old Germans, who called himself Hans, in the strongest German language. "They are pilots, not infantry soldiers, and are just trying to return to their airbase. Besides, we are being overrun by the Allied forces today. Look at us. We are not the German army. We are German citizens who *Der Führer* is willing to sacrifice so he can stay alive a few days longer. We have no chance to hold back the Allied army, let alone defeat them. If we execute these pilots, the Americans will execute us in a few days as murderers."

"He is right. Killing us will not help you win the war," Bud Sullivan said. "It will just guarantee that you will die in the near future as sacrificial lambs in the name of the defeated Third Reich."

"It is our sworn duty," the youngster replied.

The German officer said, "Ja, they must be shot, and I will do it now." He slowly unbuttoned the cover on his Lugar sidearm and drew the pistol.

The other two German guards walked through the open barn door and stood behind the officer and teenage driver. All in the barn noticed the entering soldiers, particularly the large stocky Volksstrum German who objected to our execution. His eyes lit up and his mouth and arms opened wide.

"Max," he exclaimed loudly and rushed toward one of the German soldiers that just entered the barn. His excitement and rush to the soldier caused a commotion and distraction.

This is the opportunity I need. Go for it. Now.

I reached into my back pocket and pulled out the Belgium revolver Bud gave me that morning. The folded trigger dropped in place and my finger wrapped around it. I raised my arm and aimed at the head of the German officer who now looked left, distracted by the entrance of Max. I squeezed the trigger. The shot exploded loudly in the barn and the shell hit the officer in the right temple. His head jerked to the left, his cap flew off, and he fell hard on the dirt floor at the feet of his driver.

I gritted my teeth, held my breath and concentration, and calmly aimed at the head of the young SS driver who looked up with wide eyes from the fallen officer. The second shot hit him in the center of his forehead with gruesome results. Behind the young driver stood the other soldier who came in with Max. That soldier raised his rifle, but Max and Hans were between the German and me. He could aim around them, but I didn't have a clear shot.

I moved, looking for an opening, and for a fraction of a second, I thought, *He's going to kill me first.*

Then I heard a shot from somewhere else, and the German guard fell, still holding his rifle. My eyes shifted to the sound and saw the other older Volksstrum farmer holding a smoking German automatic pistol. I froze for a moment then heard Bud's familiar voice.

"You got 'im." He rushed to pick up their weapons.

I moved my aim to Otto, but Hans and Otto both dropped their guns. Hans held Max tight so he couldn't raise his rifle in defense of his comrades. "We're going to help the Americans. They will not shoot us."

The others in Hans' group understood Bud's German commands "lass es fallen" (drop it) and "hande hoch" (hands up). The American prisoners rushed to pick up the German guns and their own from the opposite wall. We pulled the Germans together and searched all for additional weapons. I put the Belgium revolver back in my pocket. For a few moments I was stunned at what just happened. After being afraid I wouldn't survive the day, fearing for my life, I was able to seize the initiative and do what I had to do, motivated by the threat to my friends and colleagues.

Bud and I had a brief emotional reunion. "Where the hell have you been?" I said to him.

"Listen, we need to decide what's next," Bud said. "We'll have time to celebrate later. What about the farmers and Max? Do we hold them as prisoners? I say, no. Lieutenant Hunt and I talked to Hans and Otto earlier. They own this land and just want to get out of the war and go back to farming. Let's get out of here and let them have their farms back. The German army has been eliminated or driven back toward Berlin. They shouldn't be bothered and it's their land anyway. I think we can square this with Colonel Gavin to leave them alone for now."

"Agree, but what do we do with these dead Germans?" I asked.

"Let's load them in their half-track wagon and leave it somewhere," Bud said. Others agreed and we all proceeded to load the dead German soldiers, including their weapons, into the half-track truck and drive it to a big ditch about a quarter of a mile up the road. "Whoever comes through after this is all over and collects the enemy dead will pick them up."

Then, we had a conversation with Hans and Otto about staying on their farms and out of the war. We took their German weapons, leaving them their own shotgun and Mauser pistole.

The rest of us squeezed into the *Kubelwagen* for the drive back down the road to the medical station at Wesel.

On the road to the aide station, I couldn't resist pumping Bud for more information on the events of the day. I was eager to find out how the hell Bud and I ended up in the same place. "Bud, you gotta tell me how you got here. I thought you were carrying paratroops and would be back at base drinking beer by now."

"No; like you, my orders changed at the last minute, and I was assigned to a tug. It just so happens we towed your glider and another. You may have seen us take a couple of big flak hits after we released them, so we had to take her down on one . Then we got strafed by a machine gun nest after surviving a belly landing just a mile or so from here. Sergeant Bolton and his glider-riders rescued our ass. It's a good thing we towed them over here in your glider, right?"

"I knew it. You were towing us. This is Lieutenant Roy Lee Harrison. He was piloting the other glider you were towing. I heard your voice on the comm line but my pilot told me it was someone else. I watched you get hit as you pulled up in a wide turn after release and your number one engine nearly dropped off your left wing."

"Yep, that was us. The flak injured my navigator and killed our radio operator, Sergeant Campbell. We had to set her down on her belly, and with a bit of luck we only tore off one wing. Then a damn machine gun started raking us before we even got out of our seats. I took a ricochet hit in my back on my shoulder blade, not much damage and my copilot Lieutenant Hunt patched me up. Legs, this is Lieutenant Bill McCallister, an old friend from back home. We call him Mac. He was a pilot on one of the gliders we towed."

"Where is your other pilot? Didn't make it?" Bud asked.

"Yeah, turns out Flight Officer Griswold was a great pilot. I gained a lot of respect for him. He was hit by shrapnel from a flak explosion on the way in, then we lost him in a bombed-out church after we safely landed. A German tank leveled the church while he was guarding enemy prisoners."

Field aid station or hospital, WWII

18. Field Hospital at Wesel

24 March 1600 hours

THE SHORT drive to the field aide station on the outskirts of the destroyed town of Wesel took only minutes and was heavily guarded by British troops. As expected, they reacted to the sight of a German vehicle approaching. I told Jimmy to stand up and wave so they understood we were friendlies, not a threat. It worked and the soldiers directed us to stop over to one side next to a line of portable tables with an overhead cover looking like a check-in point. Behind that was a large tent I anticipated to be the triage area I visited earlier in the day and hospital for the seriously injured.

I saluted the British guards that met us and we

explained our situation. Bud, still holding on to his bloody dressings, and Lt. Coffman with his splinted leg, were immediately helped into the triage tent. Roy Lee and I stepped to the table of two medics and a doctor taking information on the injured.

"I see you've brought us some customers, Lieutenant," said one medic, a M.Sgt. who looked to be in charge.

"Yes, that's Lieutenant Bud Sullivan and Lieutenant Dan Coffman, both C-47 airmen from the French airfield at Coulommiers. Earlier today we sent you Sergeant Jenkins with a serious wound. A medic from this station came out with me to pick him up a couple of hours ago. Do you know his status? Can we see him?"

"He'll be in the hospital tent behind me. Ask for Doctor Nash or Medic Brown, who, I believe are still tending to the soldier you sent in."

We headed for the hospital tent. On entering, we immediately saw Sgt. Jenkins on a table with two medical people attending him. Across the room, near the entrance, Bud was prone on a covered table, being attended to by what looked like a doctor and a medic. I asked, "Are you Doctor Nash?"

"Yes, and don't come any closer; this is a clean surgical area. We'll be through momentarily. Lieutenant Sullivan will be fine, and you can talk to him in a few minutes."

Coffman was on another table where a doctor was re-dressing his leg. His eyes were closed. I assumed the doc gave him pain medicine.

Roy Lee and I turned away and saw a man in fatigues walk toward me from the center of the tent. As he got closer, I saw gold leaf Maj. insignia on his shoulders. I didn't recognize him until he said, "Lt. McCallister?"

For a moment, I was stunned. Then I remembered to salute. "Major Maxwell? How did you get here?"

"I rode in on a troop carrier flight and had to bail out with the paratroops after getting hit hard by the German AA guns."

"Sorry, sir, didn't mean to question you, just didn't expect to see you again. This is Lieutenant Roy Lee Harrison. He piloted our sister glider and helped us get passed several encounters with the enemy."

"As Colonel Gavin and I said, everyone in this air group would have a job to do today. That included me. Earlier today I ran into someone you know. Follow me."

We followed him back toward the rear of the tent to a soldier sitting in a wooden folding chair off to the side. His head was wrapped in a bandaged. It took me a second or two to recognize him.

Good God. It's Jerry.

"Jerry," I shouted uninhibited. "Oh my God, you're alive. I thought you were a goner after that tank blew away the remains of the church. My God. What happened? How the hell did you survive? You remember Roy Lee. He was with us in the bombed-out church."

Jerry said he decided to leave the church because there were no sounds of an attack on the tank squad. Then an explosion. "All I remember was sitting in the rubble of the church with the Kraut prisoners, the explosion, and Major Maxwell and troops waking me up after finding me unconscious in the cemetery."

"I'm so glad you're going to be OK." I reached out with both hands and took his hand. I continued, "Your encouragement and confidence in me got me through the day."

He said, "I cracked my head on one of the gravestones. I'm okay but suffered a concussion and the doctor told me to rest for a while. I guess you've had an interesting day as well, Lieutenant, and I notice you've come through this mission without as much as a scratch. As I said this morning, with you and I working as a team, we have a good chance of getting through the day."

"Gentlemen," a voice behind me called out. I stood and turned around. "Major?"

"I thought you would want to know," he said. "One of your buddy's, Lieutenant Zack Palmer's, C-47 tow plane was hit by anti-aircraft guns, lost an engine, and crashed a couple of miles into Germany. Two of his crew bailed out safely, but Lieutenant Palmer and his copilot Lieutenant Skinner perished trying to land their crippled tow plane."

"Thanks for letting us know, Major."

How many times today did I wish I was doing something different than flying a glider? Another lesson in "Be careful what you wish for!"

"You were right, Jerry, and there were others today that helped me avoid death, or serious injury, on at least a couple of occasions. I was ready to go after the tank patrol after they blew up the church with you in it. Sergeant Jenkins kept me from charging after the Krauts and maybe getting us all killed. Later, he took a sniper's bullet looking out for the rest of us just trying to get back to our rendezvous location. We finally reached a farmhouse and barn where we were captured by a couple of Volkssturm home guard Germans. It was there that I used a small revolver Bud Sullivan gave me to take out a German officer who was about to execute us all."

"You mean you killed a German today?" Jerry asked.

"Actually, more than one, and I'm not proud of it. Just glad I was able to do it at the time."

"You certainly save my bacon," Jerry said. "We would have likely crashed had you not taken over."

"Instinctive, Jerry. As I expect you know, it's like riding a bike. After you've flown as many hours as you and I have, flying is flying. Glider or bomber makes little or no difference. I admit, at the time I wasn't as confident, especially about making the dead-stick landing."

19. Return to Base

March 24 1500 hours

I SAT ON a cot next to Jerry Griswold and we continued to recall the events of the day.

Jerry said, "I guess I'm lucky I moved out of there when I did. The fact that you showed up here, Mac, suggests you had a difficult day. Where did you guys go? I thought you all were going to take out that tank squad, but I never heard a shot. Did you just decide to avoid them?"

"We did, and I was surprised. Sergeant Jenkins had decided to let them pass, instead they stopped. Our hesitation allowed them time to rotate their turret and fired into that half-wall we thought you were sitting against. Sergeant Jenkins, who made that call, was wounded by a sniper less than an hour later. Corporal Jimmy DuPree was able to take out that sniper, but a second sniper killed two of our troopers."

"Tell me more, Lieutenant. For a guy that knew he was doomed to die in the flying coffin, you managed to dodge a flak hit during landing, then dodged a fight with a tank squad, and when snipers drew a bead on your flight group, and you were the only one that came away without a scratch. Once again, I and others were glad you were the man of the hour helping all of us. One question," Jerry continued. "Did you fire your weapon today?"

"I did, Jerry, and I'm not very proud of it. It wasn't much of a fight. I would rather not re-live the details. Later, maybe, over a beer."

"What do we do now?" Jerry asked. "How do we get back to our airbase? Do you know where our pilots' rendezvous location is? I'd sure like to get out of here soon, how 'bout tomorrow."

"Yeah, I agree," I said. "But I'm not sure where that is from here, and it may have changed from the original map location, or they've hauled out some pilots and we missed the pickup. The original spot was a northwest road entrance to Wesel. We're at the western road into town. The Brits were supposed to pick up the pilots, but I believe those Operation PLUNDER ground assault people have moved on north to the Issel River."

I moved closer to Jerry, pulled up a folding chair, and sat next to him. "You just continue to rest.

I think with your injury, you could easily get a ride out of here to a Belgium hospital, when you're able to travel. The rest of us may have to hitchhike back if we don't find an empty personnel truck that will haul us. I'll talk to Major Maxwell to help us all get back to base."

I found Bud checking on his injured crew and receiving some attention to his own wound. His wound was not life threatening, but the medical staff advised him to take one of the hospital cots and rest for a day or two before trying to ride or walk the two hundred plus miles back to base. The injury needed to heal a bit before traveling.

Walking away from the medical staff, Bud said, "Behind this tent is a storage area holding additional cots and blankets. Why don't you go out there and pick one up and set up in here while we figure out how to get back to base. I'm in no hurry, are you? The food here is better than rations, and they have plenty of coffee."

I took his advice because we had few choices. Besides, I wanted to stay close to Jerry while he recovered. I got a cot and set up on the very back wall of the hospital tent, away from patients who required regular observation. The first night was a toss-and-turn period of little sleep despite my state of exhaustion. There was loud gunfire from the few remaining planes of the German *Luftwaffe* taking random night strafing shots at the two bridges over the Rhine.

The next morning, I made some inquiries

about returning to our French base. The simple answer was either "Get in line" or "You're on your own." The main bridge was a makeshift pontoon bridge built by the Army Corps of Engineers and not designed for heavy traffic. It was alternating between a one-way east route into Germany for bringing in more artillery, tanks, and troop trucks and one-way west for delivering wounded to hospitals in Belgium. The MPs designated the pontoon bridge one-way west only for transporting casualties back to larger, better-equipped, brick-and-mortar Belgian hospitals. British and American pilots had little to no organized transportation back to their base. Sadly, healthy pilots were low on the evacuation priority list.

The return of C-47 and glider pilots back across the Rhine to their home base was sporadic, disorganized, and many were left to their own resources to find their way back. Some managed to hitch a ride on troop trucks returning to France after delivering replacements. Getting back to A58 at Coulommiers, or any other base in central France, was even more dependent on luck. Hitchhiking on any friendly vehicle was popular, but a long shot. Many crews hitched a ride on the trains running from Antwerp to Brussels to Paris. From there one could walk the few miles back to Coulommiers or one of the nine airfields within a few miles of Paris. Some chose to spend a night in Paris, or two or three if their funds or gambling winnings allowed a longer stay. Those R & R hours waiting to attempt a long trek back to A58 gave Bud and me time to reflect on the previous

24 hours of hell. The next morning after some rest, we enjoyed fresh coffee and caught up on events since we split after the VARSITY briefing.

"You were angry and scared, as we all were, when assigned to pilot a glider," Bud said. "You were sure this was a suicide mission. How did you manage to get through it, to survive?"

"First, it was Jerry Griswold, who was so sure and so positive that my experience and pilot skills would allow us to survive, working as a team." I pointed my finger at Bud. "You were right. Jerry was just as you said, a damn good pilot regardless of his lack of formal training. My piloting was better than I thought it could be. Again, you were right, but the real-life lessons came after I landed that overloaded brick with wings."

Bud interrupted. "Let me guess. You found out you could fight. You fired back when shot at and attacked instead of retreating. You became a soldier today. Something you were afraid to be. Right?" "Yes. Now that you put it that way. The whole of experiences of the day changed my attitude. I found truth in the adage, you never feel more alive as when you're faced with the possibility of death. Also, I know that when your friend, your brother, is threatened, you can and will find the courage to do what it takes to help him. That feeling of being more alive happened several times in one day."

"How does it feel to be the hero of the day?"

I shook my head. "No. I'm no hero. I am pleased and comforted that I was able to do my duty, do what had to be done to get through the life-threatening events we were faced with. It's been a lesson learned about resilience, knowing you can overcome fear by facing it and working through it."

Bud reached across the dining table, almost spilling the coffee, and grabs my hand. "I'm proud of you, my friend; and God bless you for saving my life."

Bud and I made it back to Paris two days later and to the A58, Coulommiers airbase on March 28th.

The last weeks of the war were more difficult and bloodier than Gen. Eisenhower or Field Marshal Montgomery expected. The Allies suffered over 10,000 casualties but captured over 160,000 Germans, liberated 200,000 citizens, and freed 6,000 Allied POWs.

The Troop Carrier Command continued to deliver air support from most of the same airstrips involved in Operation VARSITY. The character of Bill "Mac" McCallister in this story is based on a real airman who flew 22 support missions after his participation in VARSITY from airstrip A58. These include several combat missions, ferrying German POWs, flying Allied injuries to hospitals in Paris, and ground support supply missions.

The Allied armies entered Berlin the first week of May, and on May 8, 1945, the war in Europe was over.

VARSITY remains the largest single-day

airborne assault in World War II and in history. Nearly 1600 air transports, over 1300 gliders, and 240 B24 bombers delivered almost 21,000 armed men, over 130 field artillery pieces, and 1800 tons of ammunition, supplies, and communication equipment from 23 airfields in France and England on target in four hours on that morning of 24 March 1945.

Dedicated to

2nd Lieutenant W. E. "Bill" McGinnis

Operation VARSITY, March 24, 1945

437th Troop Carrier Group, Squadron 83

CP CG-4A Glider serial 36

Coulommiers Airfield A-58

He lived this story.

References

Ammerman, Gale R. *An American Glider Pilot's Story*. Merriam Press, 2020.

Delaforce, Patrick. *Onslaught on the Hitler's Rhine: Operations PLUNDER and VARSITY March 1945*. Fonthill Limited Media, 2015.

Fenelon, James M. *Four Hours of Fury*. Simon & Schuster, 2019.

Lowden, John L. *Silent Wings at War*. Smithsonian Institute Press, 1992.

MacDonald, Charles B. *The Last Offensive*. Center of Military History, 1993.

McGaugh, Scott. *Brotherhood of the Flying Coffin*. Osprey Publishing, 2023.